Caterpillar Summer

Caterpillar Summer

Gillian McDunn

BLOOMSBURY
CHILDREN'S BOOKS
NEW YORK   LONDON   OXFORD   NEW DELHI   SYDNEY

BLOOMSBURY CHILDREN'S BOOKS
Bloomsbury Publishing Inc., part of Bloomsbury Publishing Plc
1385 Broadway, New York, NY 10018

BLOOMSBURY, BLOOMSBURY CHILDREN'S BOOKS, and the Diana logo
are trademarks of Bloomsbury Publishing Plc

First published in the United States of America in April 2019
by Bloomsbury Children's Books

Bloomsbury books may be purchased for business or promotional use. For
information on bulk purchases please contact Macmillan Corporate and
Premium Sales Department at specialmarkets@macmillan.com

Library of Congress Cataloging-in-Publication Data
Names: McDunn, Gillian, author.
Title: Caterpillar summer / by Gillian McDunn.
Description: New York : Bloomsbury, 2019.
Summary: Since her father's death, Cat has taken care of her brother, Chicken,
for their hardworking mother but while spending time with grandparents
they never knew, Cat has the chance to be a child again.
Identifiers: LCCN 2018010841 (print) | LCCN 2018017751 (e-book)
ISBN 978-1-68119-743-2 (hardcover) • ISBN 978-1-68119-744-9 (e-book)
Subjects: | CYAC: Brothers and sisters—Fiction. | Responsibility—Fiction. |
Single-parent families—Fiction. | Grandparents—Fiction. | Family
problems—Fiction. | Islands—Fiction. | Family life—North Carolina—
Fiction. | North Carolina—Fiction.
Classification: LCC PZ743453 Cat 2019 (print) | LCC PZ743453 (e-book) |
DDC [Fic]—dc23
LC record available at https://lccn.loc.gov/2018010841

Book design by Jeanette Levy
Typeset by Westchester Publishing Services
Printed and bound in the U.S.A. by Berryville Graphics Inc., Berryville, Virginia
4 6 8 10 9 7 5 3

To find out more about our authors and books visit www.bloomsbury.com and
sign up for our newsletters.

For Nora

Caterpillar Summer

PART ONE

End & Begin

You and me, me and you. We'll always be together.

—Caterpillar in *Caterpillar & Chicken: The Great Bubble-Gum Pancake*

1

Cat always kept her brother in the back of her mind, except for the times he was at the front of it.

She might be multiplying fractions in her head while her brain quietly asked, "Did you cut the tag out of Chicken's shirt?"

She might be studying plants of the tundra biome when her mind questioned whether his teacher was calling him Henry, which he hated.

She might be scooping mashed potatoes on her tray when she wondered, "Will he be the only first grader left behind at the aquarium?"

On a good day, Chicken liked to wander. On a bad day, Chicken would bolt. But no matter what, Cat loved him as wide as the Golden Gate Bridge, as deep as the sea floor, and as fierce as a shark bite.

The last day of fifth grade, Cat was on alert. Usually the last day of school was messy, noisy, and busy—the kind of day that could easily be too much for Chicken. When he got upset, he couldn't always calm himself. He got more and more tangled up until he overflowed and every feeling came rushing out. Mom called it a meltdown, but to Cat it was tight and sharp. It was the opposite of melting.

When the dismissal bell rang, Cat slid her backpack to her shoulder and hustled double-time to the steps at the entrance. The sky above her was gray and low but inside Cat felt like sunshine. She bounced on the balls of her feet. The bounces said: *summer*, *Atlanta*, and *my best friend, Rishi*. If her heart had its way, it would have skittered out of her chest and started vacation without her.

The next day, they'd fly east until they reached Atlanta. Mom would teach a three-week college class, and Cat and Chicken would tag along to see the Krishnamurthys, who moved to Georgia last summer. It had been a year, but Cat still missed going to Rishi's house to play, do homework, and eat dosas. But even from thousands of miles away, he was still her best friend.

Plus, Mom promised they would have a *real* vacation when she wasn't teaching. It would be the first Cat could remember since it was just the three of them.

A stream of kids poured onto the sidewalk, and Cat side-stepped the elbowing boys and twirling kindergartners.

"Hey, Cat," said a voice behind her.

Cat turned, expecting to see her brother—but instead, it was Poppy Zhang, the nicest girl in fifth grade. Her cheeks dimpled when she smiled, and at that moment she was dimpling at Cat.

"You crushed that geometry review," said Poppy.

Math was Cat's favorite, and geometry was her best. Cat liked geometry's rules. They made her feel organized.

"Thanks," said Cat. "You too."

Poppy laughed. "I'm not so sure, but thanks." She tilted her head toward a cluster of girls on the sidewalk. "A few of us are going to Toy Boat. Do you want to come?"

Of course Cat wanted to go. She could almost taste the mint chocolate chip. But then she thought of her brother.

"I know you watch Chicken after school," Poppy said. "You could bring him."

It would never work. He'd wiggle right off his seat. He'd drip ice cream on the table. He'd drip ice cream onto Poppy Zhang.

Cat shook her head slowly. "I can't."

Poppy looked disappointed, but offered Cat a smile. "See you around." She hurried to catch up with the others.

Most days, Cat didn't mind watching Chicken. It wasn't his fault that he needed her in the afternoon. It wasn't Mom's fault she worked all the time. It wasn't the Krishnamurthys' fault they moved to Georgia for a new job for Rishi's mom. It wasn't anyone's fault, but Cat's insides didn't feel like sunshine anymore.

"Caterpillar!"

She turned halfway before getting caught between a squeeze and a crash.

"Hey, Chicken!" She patted his back until he let go.

She leaned back to see him. He was the kind of kid who wore his day on his face. When his brown eyes crinkled in a good-day grin, she couldn't help but grin back.

Silently, he held out a clenched fist. "For you, Caterpillar."

Cat stretched out her hand to receive the daily treasure. The dandelion was wilted, but she turned it gently, like it was made of gold.

"It's beautiful." She tucked the flower in her pocket and studied his face. "Good day?"

Chicken shrugged.

Cat raised her eyebrows. The last day of school was chaotic and Chicken didn't like being off schedule. "Are you sure? No hard times?"

He frowned slightly, looking back at her. "It was loud when we cleaned our desks, but I did belly breaths until I felt calm." He inhaled deeply, rounding his stomach, then pushed the air out in a burst.

"Good job using strategies." She looked him over. Traces of frosting crusted his chin and gray paint streaked his sweatshirt, but overall he looked good. Cleaning a mess was easier than fixing a bad mood.

Down the steps he galloped, art projects and worksheets flying from his backpack like a paper tornado.

Cat sighed. Even if he'd managed the school day, he still

needed her for some things. "Hold on," she called after him, gathering his papers. "You didn't zip up."

Chicken spun, whirling more papers across the steps.

"All my work from the year," he announced.

"This is schoolwork?" Cat asked. "More like an explosion in a paper factory." She returned the pages to his backpack.

"And sharks? Don't have swim bladders?" Chicken's voice squeaked with excitement, adding question marks that shouldn't be there. Sharks were Chicken's favorite—a surprising choice for a boy who was sweet as marshmallows.

Chicken was still talking. ". . . But sharks? Have oil in their liver? Which makes them float?"

Listening to Chicken talk about sharks made Cat think about a *specific* shark. A shark they needed every night at bedtime. She rummaged in his backpack, reaching past crumpled papers until her fingers found the edges of a plastic fin. *Whew.*

She zipped the backpack. "All set."

Chicken stopped his shark chatter and turned to her. "Since I had a good day and used my strategies, can we celebrate?"

"What kind of celebration?" She thought of Poppy Zhang. "Ice cream at Toy Boat?"

Before she could finish, Chicken was already shaking his head. "I hate that place. Too many eyes watching me."

Toy Boat's shelves were crowded with vintage action figures and other old toys. Chicken didn't like all the faces. "They're just toys, Chicken."

Chicken stuck out his chin. "I want Chinese buns."

He loved the sesame-crusted buns with sweet bean paste nestled inside.

"Where is Mama working today?" Chicken asked.

Mom wrote books, taught illustration to college students, and picked up shifts at the Russian bakery. She always said three jobs plus two kids equaled one busy life. Even though she never mentioned Daddy's medical bills, Cat knew they were part of the equation, too.

"She's at home, working on her book," said Cat.

"Please can we go?" Chicken's eyes were open so wide his lashes curled to his brows. "I promise to stay out of the way when you pack."

"Deal," said Cat.

Together they walked downhill toward Clement Street. Cat gripped Chicken's hand when they crossed streets. Always, in the back of her mind, she was afraid of losing him. It had happened a few times this year, more than Cat wanted to admit. Once, he left the playground swings for the turtle pond. At the aquarium, he ditched the tide pools for the brownbanded bamboo shark. At the grocery store, he fled the spaghetti aisle for the Popsicle freezer. He was impulsive enough to be dangerous, and fast enough to travel far before anyone noticed he was gone.

Chicken tightrope-walked the curb alongside parked cars. "Guess what I did at school today." This was the game they played every day. It was what she used to play with Daddy.

"Hmmmm," Cat said, pulling her jacket around her. "Did your class have a snowball fight?"

"No!" Chicken exclaimed, giggling. "San Francisco has fog, not snow."

Cat wanted to think of something even more ridiculous so she could hear that laugh again. "Did you . . . go skydiving?"

Chicken chuckled. "No way! Guess again." They reached Geary and Chicken jabbed the crosswalk button.

"Hold my hand," Cat said.

Chicken punched the button again. "We're not crossing yet."

Cat narrowed her eyes. "This is a big street and super busy, so hold it, okay?" It was a warning, not a question.

Chicken frowned but held out his hand.

Cat squeezed. The light turned and they hustled across.

"You have one more try," Chicken reminded her. They were back on the sidewalk, but he hadn't let go. She looked at their clasped hands. Cat's skin was in between Daddy's dark skin and Mom's pale skin. Chicken's skin was a little darker, more like Daddy's.

"One more try? I better make it a good one." Cat scrunched her face. The gray paint on his sweatshirt and pages of artwork floated into her head. She opened her eyes. "I think you painted some sharks."

Chicken's eyes and mouth formed perfect Os. "How did you know?"

"Lucky guess."

He looked at her like she was a genius. She bumped him lightly with her hip.

Clement Street was known as San Francisco's "other" Chinatown. It wasn't much of a tourist destination, but it still bustled with shoppers and traffic. Chicken pushed open the bakery door, releasing a blast of warm, sweet air. Chicken jumped from square to square across the checkered linoleum floor. Cat knew he was playing the hot lava game.

Cat ordered and paid, then handed Chicken the crinkly bakery bag with three sesame buns inside. Her pineapple bun was in its own bag, which she held carefully as they walked back outside to the cool afternoon. Together they stood on the sidewalk and gazed at the wedding cake in the window. Clement Street was familiar to them, but there were always new things to see. They wandered past the Burmese restaurant, the furniture store, and the bar where Irish music played at night.

Chicken's favorite place on Clement was the fish market. He didn't like the smell, so he pinched his nose shut as they stood on the sidewalk and viewed the murky tanks.

Cat was thinking about the last day of fifth grade, which meant the first day of sixth grade was less than three months away. Chicken would be in second grade, but for the first time they'd be in different schools. This worried Cat. Her brother struggled more than most kids. Sometimes he needed the music turned down. Another time, he might need a sock seam straightened. Cat was the best at helping him, but how could she be there for him when her middle school was six blocks away?

A single lobster scrabbled in its tank, its claws banded in blue. Below, a tank of crabs brawled. A fat crab climbed across the others like it was their king. She reached over to nudge Chicken, but her elbow met empty space.

She turned. No seven-year-old boy with brown skin and curly hair. No gray backpack, no yellow-striped shirt. She looked up the block, then whirled the other way. Her stomach twisted. He was gone.

"Chicken?" she called.

A guy with rings in his ears strolled by, carrying a paper cup of coffee. He looked up from his phone to nod at the market window. "No chicken. Plenty of fish." He laughed to himself and kept walking.

Not helpful. She scowled as he passed.

In the produce market, short bananas dangled above glossy eggplant and bumpy avocados. Pale cabbages were stacked in mountains, dried roots looked like interplanetary visitors, but there was no Chicken.

To find her brother, she had to think like him. She headed down the street. Chicken loved the pizzeria that gave them balls of fresh dough to play with, but their doors were locked until dinnertime. The pharmacy was small and it took one peek to see he wasn't there. Back toward the fish market, she dodged shoppers and weaved through a group of people with piercings. A woman pulling a metal shopping cart talked loudly in Mandarin. A bus stopped and a wave of people crushed onto the sidewalk.

Cat circled back to the fish market, glancing at the shimmering fish. She felt underwater too—she couldn't breathe the air. A delivery truck roared by, rumbling her insides.

"Chicken!" she yelled. There was no answer.

When the bus pulled away from the curb, something across the street caught her eye. Outside the bookstore, a statue of a gnome-like clown guarded the bargain books with a wide smirk. Chicken had loved it since he was a baby. He called it the Book Elf.

She looked both ways, then ran across. There was no sign of him. She burst into the bookstore. A pink-haired woman was behind the counter.

"Have you seen my brother?" Cat asked.

The woman looked up. "Who's your brother?"

"He looks like me, but this high." Cat held up her hand to a spot on her ribs. "Short hair, gray backpack."

The woman shrugged. "I haven't seen any kids."

Cat was back outside in a flash. The woman called to her, but Cat kept going. No one could help her now. Her heart raced. The world swirled green and gray as tears popped in her eyes. She wiped them away. Crying wouldn't help Chicken.

And then she saw them.

On the other side of the statue, from under one of the bargain tables, there were two blue sneakers. Small ones, attached to skinny legs.

She walked over and squatted down. "Chicken."

When he looked at her, his face broke open in a smile. In one hand was a sesame bun with some bites chomped out of it. In the other was a book. "I found one of Mama's!" He held it up, the familiar caterpillar and chicken on the cover. "By Amanda Gladwell."

Cat leaned her forehead against the table. Her heart hadn't slowed, hadn't lowered itself from where it sat sideways in her throat. "Chicken. Why are you under here?"

"I was done with the fish," he explained patiently. "I went to see the Book Elf."

Cat crawled under the table, pressing against him. She leaned against the wall of the bookstore and breathed in the smell of poster paint, no-tear shampoo, and bean paste. Six sesame seeds stuck to his chin. Tears popped in her eyes again for no good reason.

She picked at one of the seeds, but it was stuck tight. "You know you can't run away."

Chicken squirmed from her fingers. "I didn't *run*. I walked."

"Oh, no," she snapped. He wouldn't get away with that. "You know what I mean—you have to stop disappearing! You could have been smashed by a car. Or you could have been taken!"

Chicken blinked slowly. He tilted his head to the side. "But I *didn't* get smashed or taken. I'm right here."

"Don't do it again," Cat said sharply. Then, more softly, "Don't run off. You scared me."

They pulled in their feet and watched a crowd of legs

walk past. She looped her hand through Chicken's backpack while he turned the pages of their mother's book. The wall was cool on her back. The book made her brother giggle. As he read, he pointed at Chicken's antics and Caterpillar's expressions.

This was what happened to the real-life things Cat and Chicken did. Mom turned them into a story, a Caterpillar & Chicken book that kids couldn't get enough of. In books, their problems were solved in a clever thirty-two pages.

Real life was more complicated. Mom counted on Cat to watch Chicken. But if Mom knew about Chicken running off, she might not let Cat watch him anymore. Then the stack of hospital bills would never get smaller. If Mom knew Chicken was disappearing, she would fall apart. Cat and Chicken were all Mom had.

Chicken traced the patterned endpapers with his small fingers. "Cat?"

She squeezed his shoulder. "Yes?"

He nodded at her hand. "Are you going to eat that?"

The pineapple bun. She handed it to him.

He took a bite and made a silly face, crossing his eyes. They laughed, huddled under the table like it was their secret cave. But even then, Cat held his shoulder. She had to keep him safe.

2

Cat grasped Chicken's hand the entire four-block walk to their apartment building. Chicken hopped up the steps one by one while Cat hunted in her backpack for the key.

Each apartment in their building had its own floor, like a layer cake. Someone had numbered the block out of order, and the building's paint was peeling, but 544 was the only home Cat had ever known. She unlocked the door. Chicken dumped his backpack and sped down the hall.

"Shhhh!" Cat whisper-shouted, pointing at the closed door of Mom's studio. "She's working."

He didn't answer. Shaking her head, she picked up his backpack and hung it on its hook.

In the living room, books were scattered on the coffee table. Plastic trains crisscrossed the country on their half-finished game of Ticket to Ride. An ivy plant suffered in the corner.

Next was Mom's studio, which she said had the best light in the apartment. Sometimes she played music or a podcast while she worked, but today was quiet.

After that was Cat and Chicken's room, where Chicken was already unloading the metal can that held his marble collection. To keep things quieter for the apartment downstairs, Mom had found a piece of carpet, but it was too big for the room. It curled along the edges of the wall like an upside-down slice of melted cheese.

The kitchen had a fake-marble vinyl floor and butter-colored counters. Pale yellow tile continued above the sink and two were painted with a little Dutch girl and boy. The girl had a pointed hat, pink cheeks, and looked straight forward. Her brother in wooden shoes was by her side.

"I bet you never lose *your* brother," Cat muttered under her breath.

A door with a rectangle of frosted glass led from the kitchen to Mom's bedroom. It had once been the dining room and was the room Cat loved best. A chandelier hung above the patchwork-quilt-covered bed. Bookshelves with stained glass doors surrounded the fireplace. The fireplace didn't work, but even the idea of it made the room cozier.

Each week, Mom helped Cat wash and braid her hair into the perfect French braid. Cat's hair took a long time to comb out, which tried both their patience. But afterward, when they sat on Mom's bed and her fingers pulled just right—not too loose and not too tight—and her hair went *slip-slip-slip* into the braid, it was the best part of Cat's week.

Some nights, after Chicken was snoring in the bottom bunk, a buttery popcorn smell came from the kitchen. She and Mom would stretch out on the patchwork quilt, with the enormous bowl between them. Mom usually picked a movie from a long time ago, when people made questionable fashion choices.

Cat would tell silly stories and Mom's big, crashing laugh warmed the room. Or Cat might whisper something awful, like the time every girl except for Cat showed up to class with their nails the same shade of lavender, from a birthday party Cat hadn't been invited to. A hug from Mom hadn't fixed it, but it had pulled Cat's heart from the bottom of the Mariana Trench to somewhere around sea level.

Mom had been working constantly, so they hadn't had a movie night in months. The most recent time, they'd stood at the window together. Cat had looked all the way past the schoolyard and the thick trees of the Presidio to the tiny red light on top of the Golden Gate Bridge.

"They turned it on tonight," Cat had said.

Mom squinted. "Turned what on?"

"The light," answered Cat. "Sometimes it's on and sometimes it's not. Tonight it's on."

"Oh, honey," she said. "That light is there every night."

Cat frowned. She knew it *wasn't* always there. Mom leaned her chin against the top of Cat's head.

"At times, the fog gets in the way," Mom continued. "But the light shines anyway, no matter what."

Mom was like that light on the bridge, Cat decided. Even when they were separated by a wall of drawings and deadlines, she was still there. The thought was enough to get Cat through anything.

She glanced at the clock, automatically adding three hours for Georgia time, wondering if she could squeeze in a video chat. Chicken's marbles were *click-click-click*ing as he sorted them into piles. Her stomach growled, the two bites of pineapple bun long forgotten, but maybe she could talk to Rishi before she made dinner.

She grabbed her tablet from the kitchen counter and clicked Rishi's name, but there was no answer. Later, she'd look over his emails, the ones that described the swimming, boating, and fishing adventures they'd have. Three weeks of glow sticks and marshmallows, three weeks of fireflies and floating in a lake under a big blue Georgia sky. Cat was up for anything.

Cat opened the fridge. Before, her dad had always cooked for the family. Cat remembered how easily the knife fit into his big hands when he chopped vegetables. One at a time, he handed her eggs to crack and mix in her own little bowl. He never minded if she got bits of shell in it. He always made her feel like her help was important.

Cat turned the stove's dial and put bread in the toaster.

Mom's studio door was still closed. Cat wouldn't miss that closed-door feeling when they were together in Georgia. She cracked the eggs and whisked them, adding salt and pepper, then poured them in the skillet and pulled out three plates. Stirring the eggs, she called to Chicken. "Peanut butter on your toast?"

"Yeah!"

She spread peanut butter and cut apples. Chicken might not touch the apple slices, but Cat would know she tried. She grabbed his favorite hot sauce, the one with the wooden cap and the picture of the lady dressed in white. Chicken had a need to put hot sauce on everything.

Chicken padded into the room. "Is Mama eating with us?"

Cat paused. "I'll check. Go wash your hands." She grabbed Mom's plate and walked down the hallway. There was a chance that Mom would eat with them, but it was more likely she'd grab a few bites while she was working.

When Cat walked into the studio, Mom looked tired. The skin under her eyes was purplish, but still, she beamed at Cat. "Hey, sweet Caterpillar."

Cat winced. She'd asked Mom to stop calling her that.

"I made eggs," she said, lifting the plate.

Mom looked apologetic. "I'm not at a good stopping point."

When Mom worked, she had a hard time changing gears, especially when there was a big deadline.

"I'll leave your food." Cat pushed aside a stack of envelopes to make a spot.

Mom reached for Cat's hand and held it. Cat looked down. Mom wore Daddy's silver wedding band on her thumb. One side was wrapped with yarn to make the finger hole smaller, so it wouldn't slip off. When he was alive, he let Cat try it on whenever she wanted. She could easily fit three of her little-girl fingers inside it. That had been a long time ago.

"Honey," Mom said. "I can tell something's wrong."

Cat's insides spun guiltily. Did Mom somehow know that Chicken had run away again?

"I think I know what's bothering you," Mom continued, rubbing her eyes. "I've been working a lot—leaning on you too much."

Cat felt extra mixed up. It wasn't right to keep secrets from Mom. On the other hand, Mom didn't need any more stress. Chicken was safe, that was what mattered.

"It's fine. I understand." The words felt thick.

But Mom was shaking her head. "I'm working hard so I can relax when we're on our trip. After I finish teaching for the day, I'll be all yours."

Mom sighed, still holding Cat's hand. "I depend on you, but I know you can handle it. You're the glue holding the three of us together."

Cat squeezed her eyes shut. The words crowded inside her. If Mom knew about Chicken wandering away, she wouldn't be so sure Cat could handle things. But she couldn't say anything, not when Mom needed Cat's help. She would tell her another time, when Mom was feeling relaxed.

Mom reached out and gave Cat a quick squeeze. Cat hugged her back.

"Tell Chicken I'll check on him soon, okay?"

Cat nodded. She shut the door gently behind her.

At the table, she gulped her eggs, which were cold, and then Chicken helped her clear the plates.

"Bath?" he asked.

Cat looked at the clock. "No time tonight. Face and teeth."

She scrubbed the dishes, then placed them in the drying rack. Chicken came out of the bathroom in jammies, shirt on backward.

"Let me see," she said.

He opened his mouth wide to show Cat. She checked behind his ears.

"Good job. Do you want a book?"

"No!" said Chicken.

Cat raised her eyebrow. "No book?"

"I don't want *a* book. I want ten books," he answered, grinning.

"One book! And only when your head touches the pillow."

He was already running, sock-feet slipping on the wood floor. She gave him a head start before chasing after him, skidding down the hall.

"I won!" he said when she came in. His blanket was pulled up to his chin and he held a Caterpillar & Chicken book, the same one he read on Clement Street.

Cat smiled. Back when Chicken was in preschool, he loved trains more than anything. This book was based on something that had really happened—Chicken had asked to go to the trains, and Mom bought tickets. At the train station, Chicken had been a bubbling-over kind of happy. But when they'd tried to board, his mood changed.

I wanted to go TO the trains.
I do not want to go ON the train.

She glanced at Chicken. He had fallen asleep as she read, gripping the plastic shark in one hand. She looked back at the final drawing, at the cloud scribbled over Caterpillar's head.

Clearly, Caterpillar was furious. In the newer books, she never got angry. She was always sweet and kind, never a bit frustrated, no matter what Chicken did.

In real life, the train day had been the opposite of funny. In the station, Chicken screamed, and Mom was the human version of a gray scribble cloud. Cat had figured out that Chicken hadn't wanted to take a trip. He'd wanted to watch the trains go by.

That's what Mom meant when she called Cat the glue. Errands, making dinner, and packing suitcases were only part of it. Cat was the problem solver, the one who knew Chicken well enough to know the difference between what he said and what he meant.

Chicken dug his bony elbow into Cat's ribs. She rolled away, listening to his slow breathing. The closet door had been flung open, probably when Chicken picked out his pajamas. She needed to pack. She'd get up and do that soon, but for now she would close her eyes. It had been a long day, and she needed a minute.

The foghorns on the Golden Gate Bridge bleated their different tones. Cat listened for the pattern. Even with the thickened summer fog, even though Cat couldn't see it, she knew the little red light glowed on.

3

Cat. *Cat.*"

The voice seemed to come from far away. Cat stirred but didn't open her eyes. Chicken was snoring, sounding like a miniature dump truck in her ear. She must have fallen asleep in his bunk last night. She shoved him lightly, hoping to stop his rumbling, then pulled the blanket over her head.

A hand shook her. "Wake up. We overslept."

The words sunk in. Cat's eyes opened wide and she jumped out of bed, crashing into Mom.

"I didn't finish packing!" Cat said.

Chicken sat up, squinting

Mom was surprisingly calm. "I'll get Chicken ready, and you pack. Deal?"

Cat nodded.

Mom held a T-shirt and soft pants. "Come on, Chicken."

He went with her and a minute later was crashing around in the bathroom, getting ready.

Cat crammed handfuls of clothes into the suitcase. They had ten minutes until the airport shuttle van arrived.

Mom called to Cat. "Have you seen my sunglasses?"

"Coffee table!" Cat hollered.

Mom's feet clacked down the hall, followed by a clunking and skittering sound. "Oops," Mom muttered. She must have tripped over the Ticket to Ride game board. Cat pictured the tiny plastic trains catching air and scattering across the room. If Chicken realized their game was messed up, he'd be upset—she hoped he wouldn't notice.

Cat tugged at the bag's zipper, which seemed to be permanently stuck. But finally it gave way and closed completely. She ran down the hall and heaved it in the direction of the front door. Next up were backpacks, which she dumped out on the floor to make space. She left yesterday's papers in a pile, but saved a notebook, a zipper case of pencils, and Chicken's heavy shark encyclopedia. They could use all of it on the plane.

Mom came out of her studio holding Chicken's tablet. "Fully charged and ready to go."

She placed it in the backpack, while Cat ran to change clothes. A thought itched in the back of her mind, but she couldn't think of what she was forgetting. She had her star earrings, curly-hair shampoo, and her favorite hoodie. She tucked away a few lollipops into a pocket, just in case.

Chicken peeked around the corner of the door. "Have you seen my shoe?"

Cat looked down. He wore baggy socks and held his left shoe in one hand. "Was it with that one?"

Chicken wiggled his toes. "Nope."

Cat sighed. "Maybe you should take them off in the same place."

He scrunched up his face. "That would be boring. I like a little mystery."

He turned and hopped down the hall. Cat shook her head. She could do with less mystery in her life, especially on a morning like this.

"Found it!" Mom called from the living room.

Cat grabbed three apples and three granola bars from the kitchen counter. Mom came through the back door, brushing her hands on her pants.

"Trash taken out," she said. "We are ready to roll."

The doorbell rang. Perfect timing. The driver took their bags and loaded them in the van.

Chicken climbed in next to an older lady with a brightly colored scarf. "You smell like flowers," he told her. She smiled thinly and looked at her phone. Chicken tried to fasten his seat belt, but his backpack was in the way.

"Wait a minute," Cat said. "Do you have your plastic shark?"

Chicken gulped. "I forgot!"

"Mom!" Cat called. "He doesn't have his shark!"

Mom ducked back inside. Cat looked sideways at the shuttle driver and Scarf Lady.

"Sorry," she explained. "We forgot something important."

The shuttle driver looked at his watch and grunted. Scarf Lady didn't respond.

Finally, Mom appeared holding the shark. Chicken clapped. Mom reached across Cat to hand the shark to Chicken, who kissed it with smacking sounds.

"Where was it?" asked Cat.

Mom shook her head, but she was smiling. "Way down under the covers, of course."

"Of course." Cat grinned back.

They had done it. Packed and out the door in ten minutes flat. When she and Mom worked as a team, they could do anything. Mom climbed into the front and chatted with the driver, who was friendlier now that they were on their way to the next stop.

On the other side of Golden Gate Park, they pulled up to a pink apartment building in the Inner Sunset, with two men waiting on the curb: one with a blond beard and one with brown skin and square glasses. While they climbed into the third row, Cat unzipped her backpack and looked inside. She hoped they would have everything they needed.

Chicken peeked over the seat at the two men behind him. "Excuse me, do you like sharks?"

His volume was about two notches higher than it should have been. Cat turned halfway so she could see the other passengers' reactions. Some people didn't get Chicken or were even annoyed by him. Especially when he was being loud in a small space.

"Indoor voice," she said quietly, so only he could hear.

Blond Beard kept his eyes locked on his phone, but Square Glasses smiled. "I love sharks," he said. "Do you have a favorite?"

"I have lots of favorites," said Chicken, leaning across the seat. "I love the dwarf lantern shark for being tiny, the cookie-cutter shark for being clever, and the whale shark for being biggest. I am going to the Georgia Aquarium tomorrow and I am going to see many, many sharks."

Cat kept an eye on the adults to see how they were reacting. Square Glasses seemed okay, and Blond Beard was neutral, still focused on his phone. Scarf Lady probably wasn't a fan. She twisted her body away from Chicken, who wiggled next to her. She was practically touching the window with her forehead. Mom, who didn't worry about these things, was chatting with the driver, who, as it turned out, had grown up in Georgia.

Cat patted Chicken's hand. "He's excited about our trip," she explained to the van passengers. "Sorry if he's bugging you."

Square Glasses smiled at Cat. "He's not bugging me. I really do like sharks."

"Do you want to see some?" Chicken asked. Before Cat could stop him, he was unzipping his bag and lugging out his shark encyclopedia.

The rest of the ride, Chicken showed his book to Square Glasses, who made admiring noises. Cat smiled to herself. Chicken had a way of picking the nicest people to talk to.

When they got to the airport, Scarf Lady was the first to wheel away her luggage.

"Have fun with the sharks," Square Glasses said to Chicken before walking away with Blond Beard.

When they checked their bags, Chicken asked how the suitcases knew which plane to get on. When they went through security, he asked about the X-ray machines. And when they were on their first flight to Chicago, he asked about everything—from how the plane worked to the clouds outside. Luckily, Mom had the middle seat and handled the questions while Cat sank into a book.

During their layover in Chicago, they got fast food. Cat gave Chicken the soft fries from her bag because he didn't like the crisp ones. He took a single bite of each and lined them up on the wrinkled burger wrapper. He picked the sesame seeds from his hamburger bun and ate them one by one.

"You should eat something besides fries and seeds," she told him.

"This food is too plain," he said.

Mom dug in her bag. Wordlessly, she removed a doll-size

bottle of hot sauce and handed it to Chicken. He shook a puddle onto the tray and dipped his burger.

Out on the runway, a plane pulled up to its gate. They were halfway to Atlanta, one plane away from Rishi.

Mom messed with her phone. "It looks like Manjula called a few times."

"Did she leave a voicemail?" asked Cat.

"She did, but I can't get a signal and I don't want to waste the charge I have left."

"Mom! Did you forget to charge it?" asked Cat.

Mom looked embarrassed. "At least I remembered to charge Chicken's tablet."

They looked at Chicken, who made *blub, blub, blub* sounds as he motored french fry boats through the hot sauce lake.

Mom put the phone back in her bag. "We'll see them in a few hours. Probably she's saying how excited she is to see you two." She patted Chicken on the head. He beamed at her.

They boarded the second flight. Chicken took the window seat and Cat was in the middle. As soon as they got in the air, Mom reclined her seat and closed her eyes.

"A million puffy clouds!" sang Chicken. He glanced at Mom. "Let's show her."

Cat shook her head. Mom needed sleep. "Maybe later. Shark show?"

"All right," he said, taking the tablet from her.

Cat had her book but was too excited to read. Silent sharks flickered on Chicken's screen as the sky turned from pink to purple to black.

When the plane started descending, Mom stirred in her seat. Cat nudged Chicken and handed him a blue raspberry lollipop. He accepted it and turned back to the window.

"Don't put your face on the glass," Cat said.

Chicken shot a look over his shoulder. "It's not glass. It's acrylic."

"You know what I mean," Cat said.

He popped the lollipop into his mouth. "Look at the lights!"

Mom squinted. "Look at the traffic."

Red brake lights and white headlights filled every inch of the road below. The plane lowered, but Cat's heart kept the clouds company. She was so close to seeing her friend.

"One of those cars has Rishi," said Chicken. "And Manjula and Sandeep, right?"

"Of course," said Cat. "Rishi can't drive himself."

Chicken twirled the lollipop in his mouth. "I'm going to play sharks with Rishi. He's my best friend."

Jealousy crackled inside her. Rishi was *her* friend. She didn't want Chicken claiming Rishi every day in endless shark games.

But maybe that wasn't fair. Rishi was Cat's friend first,

but Chicken wasn't wrong about Rishi being his friend, too. He was friends with everyone. That was the whole point of Rishi.

They'd be in Atlanta for three weeks. There would be plenty of time for Chicken to play with Rishi, and time for Cat and Rishi to hang out together, too. Vacation meant there'd be enough time with everyone—even Mom.

The plane lowered farther.

Chicken's eyes widened and he grabbed her arm. "We're still going so fast."

The landing in Atlanta was rougher than it had been in Chicago. Cat's insides pulled forward and then settled as the plane slowed.

"Whew!" Chicken said loudly, making the people around them laugh.

People in the front rows filed off the plane. Chicken looked out his window, describing the trucks with blinking lights.

Cat pulled her backpack from under the seat in front of her. "Chicken, get your bag."

"In a minute," said Chicken. "I'm watching for our suitcases."

Cat leaned over and tugged at his backpack, which was tangled under the seat. He allowed her to put it on his shoulders, but didn't take his eyes off the window.

Finally, it was their turn. Mom stood. "Come on, Chicken."

He didn't budge. Cat put her hand on his shoulder.

He shrugged her off. "I'm watching the guys!"

Cat took a deep breath. "There's more guys inside, okay? Really cool ones."

Chicken wasn't having it. "I don't want to see inside guys."

Cat leaned down and talked close to his ear. "Guess what I heard. The whole aisle is hot lava and you have to hop from one island to the next. Help me, Chicken—I don't want to fall in."

He giggled and took big steps off the plane and down the Jetway. Cat and Mom had to hurry to keep up. But his burst of energy ran out. As soon as they stepped into the terminal, he sank to the floor. People with bulky suitcases streamed around them.

He looked up at Cat. "No lava."

"Chicken, stand up," said Cat.

He kicked off his shoes.

"No, sir," Mom said, bending to gather them. *No, sir* was one of those Southern expressions Mom used when Chicken stepped way out of line. Southern people got more polite when they were mad. It didn't make any sense.

He sprawled on the floor. A man grunted as he side-stepped, almost bumping Chicken with a suitcase. A woman whispered about spoiled children. Cat's face warmed.

Mom lifted Chicken to standing and half carried him from the walkway. "You're going to get stepped on if you aren't careful."

This was fair, but Chicken wasn't in the mood for

fairness. His face crumpled in slow motion. He leaned back his head and screamed. The terminal echoed with it. Mom started doing deep breath exercises, moving her lips silently. Probably counting to fifty.

Chicken walked in tight circles, flapping his hands. The more riled up he got, the harder it was for him to calm down. If they waited for Mom to get to fifty, Chicken could be at five hundred. Cat searched his bag.

"Chicken," said Cat. "When you're done, I'll show you something."

On the outside she pretended to be calm, even though her insides jangled. If she acted patient and steady, Chicken would come around.

She pulled out the photo album, the one they called the Big Blue Book. Chicken loved their family pictures.

Turning pages, she watched him from the corner of her eye. By the fourth page he sat next to her. On the sixth page, he leaned his head against her shoulder. When she handed him the shark, he put it in his mouth.

The pictures weren't in time order. A picture of Daddy and Mom in college was next to one of Cat and Chicken last year, holding plastic Halloween pumpkins. Cat liked the pictures mixed up because Daddy was right next to them, not frozen in the time four years ago.

When she got to the end, she started over. They looked at pictures until Chicken's breath steadied.

She made her voice sweet as blue raspberry. "At the

baggage claim, we'll look at the Big Blue Book some more. Good idea?"

Chicken nodded and held out his arms for Mom. She lifted him and gave Cat a grateful nod. *Teamwork.* Cat scooped up Chicken's backpack and Mom's bag. The load was heavy, but Cat was strong.

When they reached the escalator, Mom leaned toward Cat. "Glad you remembered to pack the book. Thank you."

Mom hoisted Chicken higher. He wasn't easy to carry, even for someone as tall as Mom. His dangling feet hit Mom's legs as she walked. Cat tried to remember the feeling of being carried. She couldn't.

When they reached the baggage claim, Cat scanned for Rishi, but he wasn't there.

Mom saw her disappointment. "Probably stuck in traffic."

Cat dropped the bags into an empty seat and pulled out the Big Blue Book. Mom transferred Chicken to Cat's lap.

All his tension had drained. He snuggled in her lap, rubbing the shark's fins with his little fingers. He tried to talk through the big yawn that quivered his body. "More pictures."

She opened the book again but his eyes were already half-closed. He let out a big sigh and fell asleep in her arms. Cat gently set the book on the seat beside them.

She craned her neck to look around. Still no Rishi. Luggage tottered down the ramp and slid onto the carousel. Mom returned with their things. She dug in a suitcase pocket and pulled out a charger, then crossed to an area with outlets and plugged in the phone. Chicken startled in his sleep, arms flying, nearly punching Cat's face.

"Shh," she murmured.

It had been a long day. She felt tired down to her toes. But nothing could hold down her heart, which floated in zero gravity. She was going to see her friend, and it was going to be the best summer ever.

Mom returned. "We've had a change in plans."

Cat yawned. She moved her head so she could see—still no Rishi. "Are they almost here?"

Mom sat. "Manjula got some bad news late last night. Her mom had a stroke and is in the hospital."

"Oh, no!" Cat's eyes widened. Manjula must be sad and scared. Cat remembered the day they got the bad news about Daddy. Everything inside her pressed together and sadness rushed in. She shook her head to clear it. "So what does that mean?"

Mom sighed. "It means Manjula, Sandeep, and Rishi are on their way to India."

Cat finally understood. The Krishnamurthys weren't driving to meet them. They weren't even in the state. Instead, they were on their way across the world.

"So our vacation is pushed back a couple days," Cat said, trying to stay calm. "They'll be back before we know it."

Mom looked at her patiently. "They haven't been to India

in so long—Rishi has cousins he's never met. They'll be a few weeks, maybe a month."

Cat's heart smashed down to Earth so fast and hard, she could picture the shape of the crater it left.

"A *month*?" It came out louder than she had meant it. "What about us?"

Mom frowned. "Cat, they need to be with their family."

"We're family, too," Cat said. Hot tears sprang up in her eyes. It was unfair. They were stuck, thousands of miles from home—for nothing.

"Cat . . ." Mom's eyes were pleading.

Cat wiped her eyes on her sleeve. "Is this what the voicemails were about? You should have charged your phone."

Mom drew back, and Cat knew she had hurt her. But Mom should be more like other grown-ups. If they had found out before leaving San Francisco, they wouldn't be in this mess.

Chicken, in his sleep, whispered, "Plankton."

Mom pressed her fingertips against her eyelids. "We'll have to find a babysitter."

Did Mom think they could find a babysitter in two days? Even if they'd had notice, most regular babysitters couldn't handle Chicken. Cat would rather handle him herself.

"No way," she said.

Mom looked at her. Cat didn't have to say why it would never work, because Mom knew.

"I'm brainstorming. We're stuck and I don't know what to do." Mom bit her lip. "How about a sleepaway camp? That would be fun."

Sometimes Mom was unrealistic. Chicken couldn't handle the after-care program at school and somehow she thought he could manage three weeks of summer camp?

"I'll watch him at the Krishnamurthys' house," Cat said flatly.

Mom paused like she was thinking it over. Then she shook her head. "You do a good job watching him after school. But I'll be working all day, and some nights. I can't leave you in a place you don't know."

"Can you cancel the class? Let's go home." If she were going to have the same old summer, at least she could have it in their own apartment. She could even let herself imagine a trip to Toy Boat with Poppy Zhang.

Mom twisted the charging cord around her fingers. "I wish I could, but I can't cancel the class. Some things are set in stone." Her frown deepened. Chicken sighed in his sleep.

"I don't want a camp or a babysitter," Cat warned.

Mom took a deep breath, like she had decided something. "I have an idea. Wait here."

She stood and walked to the corner with the plugs, and faced the windows.

Cat bit the insides of her cheeks. Sometimes she wished she could be like Chicken. He wasn't bothered by what others thought. She wanted to scream and cry, too.

Mom was back, fiddling with the phone like she was nervous. "New plan. You'll stay with your grandparents."

Cat's grandparents lived in St. Louis. She wouldn't mind visiting them. Maybe they could go to a Cardinals game. But St. Louis wasn't exactly next door to Atlanta.

"We're going to see Granny and Pop?" Cat asked.

"Not Daddy's parents," Mom said grimly. "Mine. In North Carolina."

Mom's parents? *Mom's* parents? In *North Carolina?* Cat frowned. She didn't know Mom's parents, she had never even met them. Cat had quit asking because Mom met every question with a tight-lipped smile and vague answers. But now she and her brother were going to spend three weeks with them. Cat didn't know what Mom was thinking.

Mom nudged Chicken out of sleep. His eyes opened halfway and he smiled a loopy grin, reaching up to her. Mom lifted him to her shoulder and grabbed a wheeled suitcase.

"But Mom," Cat started.

Mom didn't listen. She nodded toward an exit. "We'll get a car out there."

Cat hurried to keep up, lugging the bags with her. The feeling of being a team with Mom was gone. Mom was in charge and she was stuck on her plan.

Cat wondered, again, what happened to make Mom stop talking to her parents. It must have been terrible. But then again, Mom was willing to drop Cat and Chicken with them. Would she do that if she really thought her parents were so bad?

Cat wondered if they had Southern accents, like the one that popped out when Mom got mad. They must know about Cat and her brother, but how much did they know about Chicken? Did they know about the meltdowns?

Fully awake, Chicken peered over Mom's shoulder, eyes round and serious. He didn't know what was ahead, and neither did Cat. But she would keep him safe, no matter what happened. That's what sisters were for.

4

On the new scale of vacation disasters, the morning had only registered slightly. Chicken cried about missing Rishi's family and the whale sharks at the Georgia Aquarium. It was a sad morning and a quiet car ride.

But after lunch, Cat's disappointment had been pushed aside by a squirmy feeling. Last night, she felt shocked that Mom would leave them with grandparents they'd never met. On the drive, shock had turned to nervousness. They would be there in a couple hours.

She popped open flaming hot cheese crackers and handed them to Chicken. Chicken read his shark book while he ate, leaving a trail of orange fingerprints on each page.

"Mom," said Cat. "This place is weird."

Mom laughed a tiny bit. "What do you mean?"

Cat gestured out the window. "Trees, trees, trees. I never knew there were so many shades of green."

"Deciduous," said Chicken, eyes still on his book.

"It's nice to see trees. We're driving through a forest, you know." Mom sounded amused.

"Evergreen," Chicken mumbled.

"Trees are fine—nothing *but* trees is weird," said Cat. "It's been like this for hours. No houses. No businesses. Even that chicken sandwich place at lunch—I couldn't see it from the freeway. For all I know, you're driving us in a big circle."

"*Highway*, not freeway," said Mom. "And 'that chicken place' was one of my four major food groups growing up."

"At the chicken place, that lady asked if you were our mom," said Chicken. He turned a page, not looking up.

Mom glanced at Chicken in the rearview mirror. "Yes, she did."

"I know why it happened," said Chicken. "It's because our skin is different colors."

"Yes, baby, that's right. But we're all part of the same family." It was the same line Mom had said since Cat could remember.

Chicken traced a life-size picture of a megalodon tooth. He didn't answer.

Cat tried to find a position where the seat belt wouldn't rub her neck. "Do your parents live in the woods?"

"No," said Mom. "They live on an island."

"An island!" said Cat. She hadn't pictured that at all.

Chicken looked up for this. "By the actual ocean? With sharks?"

Mom smiled. "Yes to both. An actual island in an actual ocean—Gingerbread Island."

"*Gingerbread* Island? Are you serious?" Cat pictured a gumdrop-covered house by a sea of frosting.

"Not the gingerbread you eat. Gingerbread is the name for the carving and scrollwork that decorated the hulls of pirate ships," said Mom.

Cat scowled. It was not the time for silliness. "Pirate ships? Mom. *Stop.*"

Mom laughed again. "I'm serious. A long time ago, there were pirates everywhere on the North Carolina coast. Your grandfather could tell you the stories."

Chicken muttered, "Cookiecutter, blacktip reef, white-tip reef, tiger, lemon, whale, hammerhead, cookiecutter, sharpnose—"

"You said 'cookiecutter' twice," Cat pointed out.

"It's one of my favorites," said Chicken happily. "The cookiecutter shark is part of the dogfish family and loves warm water. It takes circular bites out of its prey so it looks like a cookie cutter has been pushed into the other fish all over. It likes a snack," he chortled. He held up his book, which showed a fish attacked by a cookiecutter shark. The fish was missing neat round circles of flesh.

"I don't think the fish finds it funny," said Cat.

"Sharpnose sevengill, cookiecutter, great white, dwarf

lantern, nurse, goblin, cookiecutter, basking." Chicken was back in his own world.

"Mom, what do we call them?" Cat asked. Her dad's parents were Granny and Pop, names given from Cat's older cousins when they were babies. She definitely couldn't call Mom's parents Granny and Pop.

"Your grandparents? How about 'Grandma' and 'Grandpa'?"

It would be weird to call strangers by grandparent names. "What are their real names?"

Mom couldn't get the car's sun visor right. She muttered under her breath and adjusted it until it clicked. Then, louder, she said, "Their names are Macon and Lily Stone."

"Macon and Lily," Cat repeated. "I guess that's better than Mr. and Mrs. Stone."

"*Doctor* and Mrs. Stone," said Mom, drumming her fingers on the steering wheel. "He was a doctor. A surgeon."

"A surgeon!" said Cat. She never would have imagined a doctor—not when Mom about passed out every time Cat or Chicken got a skinned knee. "What are they like?"

"Mom is sweet, she's excited to see you. Dad won't be around much, I'm sure." The road curved past a field of purple wildflowers.

Cat wished Mom would say what she meant. Cat knew nothing about these people and yet she was supposed to spend weeks there without complaining.

"What's the deal anyway? Why don't you ever talk about them? Why don't you ever talk *to* them?" Cat asked.

Mom caught Cat's eye in the rearview mirror and then looked back at the road quickly. "Actually," she said quietly, "I do."

"*What?* You talk to them?" Cat had never heard Mom on the phone with them.

"I talk to my mom." Her words came out in a rush, like if she said them quickly they could move to another topic.

Cat's heart whooshed like a deflating balloon. Anger rushed out and hurt settled in. She couldn't understand it. Mom talked to them, these people she never bothered to tell Cat and Chicken one thing about.

She wondered what else she didn't know. "Did I meet them when I was a baby?"

"No," Mom answered. Cat waited. Chicken turned a page.

Then Mom cleared her throat. "We had a big argument a long time ago, around the time I finished college. My dad wasn't happy with my plans for my future."

Questions sprang to Cat's head. Maybe they'd been mad about Mom moving. Or unhappy about her marrying Daddy. "What does that mean?"

Mom tapped her fingers on the steering wheel. "They thought I was too young to know what I wanted," she said finally. "But mostly, they couldn't understand that the life I wanted looked so different from theirs."

Cat didn't think of Mom as young, but she was fifteen whole years younger than Rishi's parents, and younger than almost all the parents at her school. Cat didn't know why that would make Mom's parents mad.

Chicken looked up from his book. "I hope I get to see a shark in our grandparents' ocean."

Mom grinned at him in the mirror. "I hope you don't!"

"Lots of them," said Chicken. "Real ones. Maybe a whale shark."

Their discussion continued, covering whether whale sharks lived in that part of the world, and whether they swam close to shore or preferred the open sea. Mom tried to circle back to the lesson that seeing sharks up close was a bad idea. She and Chicken had different opinions on this topic.

Cat wanted to turn the conversation back to her grand-parents, but it was impossible to derail the hundredth round of Sharks: Friends or Enemies. She couldn't shake the feeling that Mom was hiding something. Cat couldn't imagine an argument that would split up a family. When it came to Mom or Chicken, Cat could never stay mad for long. What kind of fight would make someone leave their parents and never come back?

When they were close to the island, Mom rolled down the windows and breathed in deep. "Do you smell it?"

Cat and Chicken looked at each other.

"Mom?" said Cat. "We've smelled ocean air before. We're from San Francisco, remember?"

Mom shook her head. "It's different here, I swear it."

Cat and Chicken breathed. It smelled . . . salty.

Mom peeked into the back seat and broke into a big smile. "Wow, I missed that!"

A red light flashed up ahead. Cat leaned forward, frowning. "Why are we stopping?"

"The swing bridge is about to open," said Mom.

Chicken wiggled out of his seat belt. "I want to see! What's a swing bridge?"

"It's like a drawbridge. But instead of opening on top, like a drawbridge does, it swings to the side. Listen—do you hear it?"

The sound was part roar, part groan. It was LOUD and seemed to go on and on. It made the inside of Cat's ears vibrate.

Chicken clapped his hands over his ears. "Too creaky!"

"Mom!" Cat exclaimed. "It sounds like it could fall in the ocean at any second."

Mom smiled. "It's a swing bridge! No need to get your feathers ruffled."

Feathers ruffled? Cat and Chicken looked at each other again. Mom's Southern expressions usually popped up only when she was really mad. She didn't seem mad now. But maybe the miles of forest, the smell of ocean air, and the creaking bridge were getting to her.

After the bridge swung back into place, they crossed to the island. It didn't creak when they drove on it. Below, the water was wide and blue, and there were different kinds of boats.

"Is this the ocean? Why aren't there waves?" asked Cat.

"It's the sound," said Mom. "The ocean is on the other side of the island. You'll get a peek right in a minute."

Chicken leaned forward in his seat. "Where are the sharks?"

"You have a one-track mind, you know that?" Cat asked.

He looked at her seriously. "I *do* know that, Caterpillar. I like my mind that way."

Mom laughed. "There are likely sharks in the sound, Chicken. And also in the ocean, but I hope they keep their distance."

They turned from the bridge onto Ocean Road and passed a row of tiny shops in a square.

"Is this it?" asked Cat. "Was that the whole town?"

Mom smiled to herself. "That is most definitely the whole town."

The houses were painted in Easter egg colors. They stood on stilts, with cars parked beneath them. Cat caught quick glimpses of the ocean, but mostly the houses and dunes blocked the view from the road.

After a few blocks, a house that towered over the others came into view. Cat leaned forward in her seat, studying it. The building looked familiar, but how could that be true when Cat had never been to this island?

Mom made a sharp right into the driveway. The house

was cool gray with white trim and sat against a ridge of dunes. She could hear the waves—and the salt smell was strong. The back of the house had a big white wooden staircase that faced the driveway, where a Jeep and a station wagon were parked. Cat tilted her head way back to see four stories of house, as big as their apartment building. Staircases leading to decks and porches encircled each level.

"I know this place," said Chicken. "This is Caterpillar and Chicken's house in *Revenge of the Pirate Yetis*."

Cat blinked. He was right. She'd read that book so many times and never knew Mom had drawn her own house. She wondered why Mom had never told them. It was like getting left out of a joke. It was the same feeling as everyone having lavender-painted nails but her.

Mom's smile widened. "This is the house I grew up in."

They got out of the car, and Chicken held Cat's hand. A gleaming wooden sign read The Stone House.

Mom saw Cat looking at the sign. "That's been there since I can remember," she said. "Everything is exactly the same."

A screen door smacked shut and a man and a woman came down the stairs.

The woman—*Lily*—wrapped her arms all the way around Mom. "Sweet girl!" They looked alike—both tall and bendy, although Lily's hair was straight silver and Mom's was wavy blond.

Macon stood to the side, not willowy at all—more like a

brick with the corners chopped off. His tanned face was wrinkled and rough and he didn't look like any doctor Cat had ever seen. She couldn't imagine him fitting in one of those white coats.

He noticed Cat looking but didn't say anything. He nodded, pushing a faded blue ball cap low on his head. He looked grumpy—the kind of grumpy that could cause someone to leave and never come back.

Lily reached for Cat and Chicken, touching their faces. Her hands were cool and smelled of oranges.

Her eyes were bright and wet. "Catherine and Henry."

Chicken pushed his head into Cat's side. "Chicken," he said, muffled against her shirt.

"Welcome," said Lily. She tucked a piece of hair behind her ear nervously.

Cat had to be polite, but she didn't have to act excited. "Nice to meet you, Lily."

If she was expecting to be called Grandma or something, she didn't let it show.

"My heart is overflowing," said Lily. "Let's go upstairs and settle in." She put her arm around Mom again and they headed to the stairs.

Cat and Chicken were left behind with Macon. Cat didn't know what to do. Macon cleared his throat. "Y'all can help me unload the car."

Macon fished something out of his pocket and walked to a small door. He put in a key and pressed a button.

"We have a small elevator," he explained. "We don't use it much except for groceries. And for the suitcases of last-minute visitors."

He didn't call them his grandchildren, he called them *last-minute visitors*. He probably wasn't any happier about their visit than Cat was.

Cat and Chicken had never seen a house elevator before. It was small but impressive. It managed to fit the three of them, along with the luggage.

In silence, they rode to the main floor. When the doors opened, Macon pulled the suitcases into a narrow hallway. He locked the door and carefully hung the elevator key on the row of hooks by the refrigerator. Cat thought he would offer to take the suitcases to the bedrooms, but he didn't. He went out the kitchen door and tromped down the stairs.

Chicken unpeeled from Cat's side and crossed to the living room window. Cat followed, mostly to keep an eye on Chicken. She'd seen the ocean before, after all.

But when she stepped in front of the glass—wow!

Her first thought was that she was wrong. The Atlantic Ocean *was* different from the Pacific—no pretty cliffs or rugged coast, just white sand rolling into green waves that glowed in the sun. At the horizon, the color deepened to a thin rim of blue. Over the edge of the deck, past the sandy dunes with feathery, stalky plants, Cat could see for miles.

A squadron of pelicans glided inches above the surface of the water. Except for birds, and a few scattered people, the beach was empty. It was as if it belonged to them alone.

"Would you like to see your rooms?" Lily asked. She glanced at Mom. "I thought I'd put Cat in your old room, Amanda. It's the same as when you left. Would you like to come see?"

Mom looked uncomfortable. "I think I'll freshen up after the drive." She disappeared into the first-floor bathroom and Cat heard water running.

Lily nodded. "I think we can manage." They each took a bag upstairs. Lily gestured to a door and Cat stepped inside. She drew in her breath when she saw it.

It was beautiful and spacious, with walls of the palest gray-green, a wide-planked wood floor, a fluffy rug by the bed. Best of all was a window seat tucked in between cubby shelves bursting with shells, books, and other treasures. The window was enormous and looked out on the ocean. Cat didn't know where to look.

Chicken flung his backpack on the bed. "This is good," he said, as if it were all settled.

"I have a guest room right next door that I thought you might like, Chicken," said Lily. "There's a blue quilt in there and you can see the ocean from that window, too."

"Nah," he said, flopping on the bed. "I'm good here."

Cat's excitement faded. Of course he wouldn't want to sleep in a new place without her.

"It's okay," she said. "We can share."

Lily looked back and forth between Cat and Chicken like she didn't know what to do. Finally, she turned to Chicken.

"Let's unpack your things in the other room, even if you sleep in here. Plus, there's something special in there I want to show you."

"All right," said Chicken. "But I'm still going to sleep here."

They left and Cat looked around. She should unpack, but she wanted to treasure the moment of being in the room all by herself. The window seat was welcoming with its squashy pillows. She stared out the window, losing herself in the curling waves.

Chicken ran back into the room with a shout.

Cat pulled herself away from the view and looked at him closely. "What are you holding?"

"I found the special thing," he crowed. "A sea turtle night-light!"

"Be careful," Cat said. "You don't want to break it."

He frowned deeply. "I just wanted to show you."

She examined the turtle, which was made of milky glass. "It's so pretty. And fragile, so *be careful*."

"I know! I'm putting it back." He ran out of the room.

Cat unpacked quickly and sat on the soft bed. The quilt was similar to the one they had back home, but the colors on this one were deep blue and coral orange. The bed was stacked with pillows. She took her satin pillowcase and was stuffing it with one of the pillows when Lily popped her head in the doorway.

Her forehead wrinkled in worry. "Did I forget to put the pillows in their cases?"

"Um." She didn't want to explain but felt she had to. "Cotton pillowcases make my hair too dry, so I use this one instead."

The concern cleared from Lily's face. "You're fine. Make yourself at home. It looks so soft, I might have to get one, too."

They shared a small smile, interrupted only when Chicken bolted back into the room.

"Mom says we're going to the beach!" he shouted before running off again.

Cat wanted to stay in her room to examine the drawings on the wall, to sit in the window seat some more. But there would be time for that later.

When they went downstairs, Chicken was pressing his face to the big window, cupping his hands against the sun. He pointed to a path that stretched in both directions as far as they could see. "Where does that go?" Smudges of orange cracker dust showed where his hands had been.

Cat wiped at the glass. She had a feeling she'd be following behind Chicken erasing the messes he made in this tidy house.

"That way goes to the pier," Lily said. "That way goes back to the shops you probably saw when you drove in."

"I want to see," said Chicken. "Let's go, let's go!"

Mom hesitated. "You'll have to watch him, Mom. He can't swim, and sometimes he takes off running."

Lily nodded, already opening the door. "Kick off your shoes first—sand in your sneakers is no fun, is it, Chicken? Would you like to hold my hand while we go out?"

Lily spoke in a way that suggested a big adventure right outside the door. Cat wasn't sure how Chicken would react, but he grabbed Lily's hand like they were old friends. Chicken's hands were both sticky and cracker-crumby, but Lily didn't pull back. Together they trooped toward the door.

"Onward," said Lily. Mom followed.

Cat glanced to see if Macon had returned, but he wasn't there. She had to admit that Lily was good at talking to Chicken, who didn't usually trust new people right away. But talking was one thing, action was another. Every minute Chicken was on the beach he would need Cat nearby, ready to react when he needed her.

The sand sizzled Cat's feet but she kept walking. She wanted to cool her feet in that glowing green ocean. Finally, she reached the water. When the wave came, she braced herself for the freezing sensation she knew from the waves at Ocean Beach back home, but the cold feeling never came. She looked at her feet in amazement.

"It's warm!" said Cat.

Mom dipped a foot. "Not bad. It will be even better in a few weeks."

Cat looked around. "I can't believe you grew up on an island."

"It's beautiful, isn't it? Oooh!" Mom reached down and grabbed something from the sand, pinching it between her fingers. "Shark tooth!"

Mom passed it to her. It was shiny black, smaller than Cat's fingernail and hard like a stone. "This came from a shark? Why is it black?"

"It's a fossil," Mom answered. "Thousands of years old."

The tooth rolled in her hand. How strange that it had once been a part of a shark's mouth. One end was rounded, where it had met the gum line. The pointed side had a jagged edge for biting. Cat was about to ask what type of shark it was from, but Mom plucked it from her hand.

"I've got to show Chicken," she said. She sprinted the short distance to Chicken, who clung to Lily. "He's afraid of the waves," Lily told Mom as she approached.

Mom said, "Honestly, that'll probably make your life easier." She and Lily smiled at each other. Mom bent down to show Chicken the tooth. Cat could still feel that shark tooth in her hand. She hadn't been ready to let it go.

Cat hugged herself against the breeze. The feeling of being a team with her mom had slipped away since yesterday, when Mom announced her plan. And now, even though they stood on the same beach, Cat felt like they were a hundred miles apart.

From a distance, the ocean seemed peaceful, but up close the waves smashed the sand. The water made the island more dangerous for Chicken—even more dangerous than busy Clement Street.

After some time on the beach, Mom looked at her watch, and then they walked up to the house. Chicken clutched the shark tooth.

When they went inside, Cat looked around the living room. Going up the stairs were pictures of Mom from each grade, frozen in time, from kindergartner with a huge bow on her head to a graduating senior. Then the pictures stopped there, at the top stair, like that girl had vanished, which, in a way, she had.

Lily stood in the kitchen. "What can I get you all to eat?"

"I should be going," said Mom.

Lily's smile sagged. "Back to Atlanta already? At least let me pack you up some snacks and tea to go."

Hot tea on a summer day sounded terrible, but Lily opened the fridge and pulled out a pitcher. "It's half-sweet, how you like it."

"Iced tea would be great," said Mom. "Thanks."

"I'll get your dad out of his workshop. He'll want to say good-bye." Lily hurried down the steps to the shed-like building Cat noticed before.

Mom turned to Cat for a hug. "Love you bunches."

"I'll miss you," Cat said.

Mom pulled back. "Me too. But I'll visit next weekend."

She didn't want Mom to leave, didn't want to be left in

this house with Chicken and two strangers. "Don't go," she said quietly, but Mom didn't hear her. She had moved on to Chicken.

"I love you, little Chicken," said Mom. "Make sure you listen to your grandparents and to Caterpillar. No ocean!"

He giggled. Mom gave him a look that was all sunbeams. Cat stood to the side.

Macon and Lily came back upstairs. Lily hugged Mom, who hugged her back, saying good-bye.

Mom scooted away before Macon could say or do anything, although Cat wasn't sure if he would have anyway. He seemed to be the opposite of Lily, at least where friendliness was concerned.

Lily, Cat, and Chicken waved from the side deck as Mom backed up onto Ocean Road. She honked the horn and then drove away.

"That's that," said Lily. "Now let's have some biscuits."

PART TWO
Bad & Good

New things can be scary, but they can also be fun.

—Caterpillar in *Caterpillar & Chicken: The Nervous Narwhal*

5

Chicken rolled over and kicked her in the side. "Do you smell that?"

Cat blinked for a moment before answering. But then her brain caught up to nose. A warm and buttery scent filled the room.

Chicken leaped out of bed and grabbed at her arms until she followed him downstairs.

"Good morning." Lily pulled a tray of biscuits from the oven.

Chicken went through five before he spoke again. "These are the best things I've ever eaten."

Lily smiled wide. "We'll have them every day if you like."

"Yes, please," he said around a mouthful of biscuit.

"That's enough, Chicken," said Cat. "Save some for Macon."

Lily waved her hand. "Never has anything but coffee in the morning until he's back from his morning walk."

Cat looked out the window. "Is he on the beach?"

"Every day, rain or shine," Lily answered.

Cat cleared her plate and Chicken's, too, but Lily scooped them away. "I'm happy to do the dishes."

Cat stood awkwardly. "Can I help?"

"Why don't you look around a bit?" Lily asked. "This is your home for the next three weeks."

Cat followed Chicken to the living room window. Yesterday's green glow was gone. The ocean was flat and gray under a thick layer of clouds.

Chicken examined the bookshelf. "They have all of Mama's books!"

He was right. The Caterpillar & Chicken books lined a low shelf in a cheerful row. Lily must have bought them—or maybe Mom sent them. Cat was certain Macon had never read one. Did Lily know they were about Cat and her brother?

Nearby on the floor a green plastic laundry basket held clean laundry inside. Chicken dumped the basket, then filled it with books from the shelf.

"This is my boat," he said. He hopped in the basket and began paging through a book.

Cat looked at him, shocked. "Chicken! You can't do that!" She didn't want Lily to think he had no manners.

"I don't mind a bit," said Lily. "I want you to make yourselves comfortable."

Cat gathered the towels and refolded them. At the top of the bookshelf was a row of golden trophies. They were different from Rishi's soccer trophies and it took her a moment to realize why. They were *fishing* trophies, each topped with a fish. Golden plates were engraved with the year and AMANDA STONE. They were Mom's!

"Lily?" Cat asked. "Was Mom into fishing?"

Lily looked up from the sink. "Oh, yes—as a girl she loved to fish. Our freezer was always full to bursting—we could never keep up with her."

"She's never taken us," said Cat. She'd never even mentioned it. Not even when Cat told her about Rishi's fishing plans.

Lily put down the dish she was holding. "Would you like to see some pictures?"

Cat nodded. Lily pulled out a thick album with a fabric cover, much tidier than the battered Big Blue Book Chicken loved so much.

They sat on the sofa, slowly turning pages. Cat had never seen so many pictures of Mom. She looked so fancy in dresses that were monogrammed, embroidered, covered in flowers. A different dress in each picture and with a giant hair bow on her head.

But when she wasn't dressed up fancy, she was fishing. Fishing! Cat still couldn't believe it. At age four or five, in pink rubber boots that were up to her knees, holding a fish as big as she was. In pigtails, standing on a pier holding three smaller fish, with Macon's hand on her shoulder, both of them grinning like crazy. Throughout elementary school and middle school, getting older, hair getting longer, sometimes in a ponytail and sometimes in loose curls. Fishing, fishing, fishing.

Cat turned the pages. "She never told us about this."

After Amanda got to high school, the fishing pictures stopped. Cat paused at a fancy picture—a group of teenagers in white dresses, wearing gloves and holding bouquets of flowers.

"What is this?"

"The debutante ball," said Lily. "With her friends. This is her." She tapped one of the figures in the picture, but Cat had already spotted her in a fluffy, layered dress.

"Fancy," said Cat. It was hard to believe Mom ever picked that, since she was one of the most yoga-pants-wearing people Cat had ever known. "What's a debutante ball?"

"It's a way of celebrating a girl becoming an adult." Lily smiled, remembering. "It wasn't exactly Amanda's style, but Macon wanted it for her. She wanted to make him happy."

So Mom had loved Macon, at least when she was a girl. Cat turned the page, showing a picture of Mom in the same dress, posing with Lily in sky blue.

"Why aren't there any pictures of Macon that day?"

A frown passed over Lily's face. "He was called in on an emergency surgery and he couldn't avoid going in. She was so upset he missed it."

Mom was pretty, but in this picture her eyes seemed flat. There was a squareness to her jaw, a look Cat recognized from the times Mom had made up her mind and there would be no changing it.

Cat flipped pages until she returned to the girl in pigtails, who looked the kind of happy that came easy. Macon was grinning, too. There was something familiar about the picture that Cat couldn't place, but then she realized it. They looked like a team. Cat felt a pang.

Cat wanted to find out what happened all those years ago. She turned pages again. The scrappy kid in boots didn't match the teenager in a bouncy white dress. It felt like something was missing. It looked like Mom had a good childhood. She grew up in a beautiful house, with the ocean in her backyard. She went fishing with her dad, and had lots of friends. To Cat, it looked like the perfect life, one Cat would give anything to have.

Something had caused Mom to turn away from Gingerbread Island. Cat needed to find the hidden story, the bits and pieces that wouldn't show up in a photo album. She could talk to Lily and possibly Macon. In a small town like this, she could find other people who knew Mom. She wanted to know why Mom stayed away for so long . . . she wanted to understand.

Cat had an ocean of questions. She hoped the island would answer.

6

Cat's favorite spot in the house was her bedroom—Mom's old room. If the house was something out of a picture book, the room was something out of a dream.

The big bed was snuggly and safe, even though she had to share it with Chicken. The walls were lined with detailed drawings of maps and ships. They were the kind of drawings that invited you in. Cat imagined Lily picking them out and framing them. Mom must have loved looking at them, too.

Cat looked for clues everywhere. So far, all she found out was that Mom had been a collector. Her treasures included shells and shark teeth, a telescope, three bunny night-lights (why, Mom?), and a million colored pencils in every shade. It was perfect, and for these three weeks, it was hers—and Chicken's, at least at night.

Downstairs, Lily was straightening the kitchen. Chicken was drawing at the table.

"Can we go out on the beach again?" Cat asked.

As she spoke, the door opened and Macon was standing on the deck, shaking the sand off his shoes. He held a blue coffee mug in one hand and a few pieces of trash in the other.

"How was it?" Lily asked.

"Good."

"Any action to report?" Lily asked.

"No action," he said. He threw away the trash and started washing his hands in the kitchen sink.

Lily saw Cat's curious expression and smiled. "Sea turtles. He looks for their nests."

Chicken's eyes widened. "There are sea turtles on the beach?"

"This time of year they make nests in the sand," said Lily. "We have to keep the lights off at night, so they can find their way back to the ocean."

"Let's go find a nest," Chicken said.

Lily patted Chicken's shoulder. "We can't investigate the nests, because that could hurt the baby turtles. But we can go for a walk after a bit. I need a little time to get ready." She glanced at Macon.

"Ah," said Macon. "I was going to work on my keel and rudder."

"Well, for goodness' sake," said Lily. "If it can't wait, bring your ship upstairs."

Macon disappeared out the door.

"I can watch Chicken if he doesn't want to be up here—" Cat started to say, but Lily had already gone to get ready. Cat felt awkward, like she had about doing the dishes. She didn't understand the rules here. Maybe she should tell them that she could watch Chicken—she watched him all the time!

She looked at Chicken. "Did Macon say he was going to work on a ship?"

"That's what he said," said Chicken, still drawing.

"And he's going to bring it up here?"

"That's what Lily said," said Chicken, switching to orange.

"Well, how is that going to work?"

Chicken didn't look up. He drew the fin of a hammerhead.

Cat looked at the page. "Sharks don't have orange fins."

Chicken shrugged. "This one does."

The door opened and Macon came in, holding some pieces of wood in one hand and a glass bottle in the other.

"Thought you might like a look at this." Macon placed the bottle sideways on the table. Inside was a tiny ship.

"Whoa!" Chicken dropped his crayon. "These are like the ones in the guest room. Do you make them?"

"I do," said Macon.

"How?" asked Cat.

"I learned by using kits, but now I make pieces from scrap wood."

Cat leaned forward. It didn't look like it had been made out of scraps. It had two masts with two big sails and a few smaller sails. The base of the boat was painted a rich navy blue and there were little portholes and even a tiny anchor.

"Do you ever go fishing on boats?" Cat asked. "Real ones, I mean."

Macon's face tensed. "No. I get seasick."

It was hard to believe that such a solid person would do something like get seasick. The thought made her want to smile a little, like when she saw a really tall person walking a tiny dog.

Macon cleared his throat. "Your mom always liked boats, but I get sick every time. I'm meant to be on land, I guess." He looked down. Cat didn't feel like smiling anymore.

Macon stood so quickly, his chair scraped the floor. "I have an errand to do. Your grandmother should be down-stairs soon." He gathered his things and was out the door before Cat or Chicken could say a word.

She didn't understand what made him bolt, just as they were having a real conversation. Watching the blue Jeep back out of the driveway made her realize how alone she and Chicken were on this island. Macon and Lily were techni-cally their grandparents, but they were also strangers. Macon seemed happy to keep it that way.

Chicken looked upset. "Was Macon mad?"

Cat's sadness turned to irritation. She couldn't stand people who made Chicken feel worried.

"I guess he had to go. Grown-up stuff." It was all she could think of to say.

"He should use belly breaths to stay calm," said Chicken. He handed her fuchsia. "Want to draw?"

She drew a starfish and filled it in until Lily came downstairs.

"Ready to go out?" she asked. She carried three rolled towels and showed them a mesh bag of sand toys. Together they headed to the sand. Sunshine danced on the waves.

"Walk first or castles first?" asked Lily.

"Let's walk," said Cat, as Chicken said: "CASTLES."

Lily looked at both of them. Cat was about to say that it was okay to build, she could wait for her walk.

"Let's walk," said Lily finally. "I want to find some sea glass for my collection. Do you want to start a collection, too, Chicken?"

Chicken nodded, with a glint in his eye. "Shark teeth."

Of course. Lily held Chicken's hand carefully and they walked toward the water.

"I don't like the waves!" he said, digging in his feet.

"We won't go in, but if we want to find shark teeth we should get closer," Lily said.

Chicken closed his eyes. Cat could tell his insides were battling—ocean-fear versus shark-love. He opened his eyes and blinked in the bright sun.

"We can look for shark teeth," he said finally. "But I don't want to get wet."

They approached the water, Chicken finding shells and rocks with each step. He handed each to Lily.

Cat paused, turning to where water met sand. There were so many shells, she had to be careful where she stepped. She checked again to make sure Lily was holding his hand. She was. Chicken pointed at the water, talking animatedly while Lily listened patiently.

The water was cooler than yesterday. She waded to her knees, watching choppy waves rush around her legs. A family of five pelicans soared over the water.

Cat wanted a do-over. She felt betrayed by Chicken for seeming so comfortable and happy here. He had been looking forward to seeing Rishi almost as much as Cat. She didn't want to let go of the vacation that should have happened. She wanted the green lake with friends who were like family—the one where she got to see Mom every night. Not dumped here with people she barely knew.

A wave bubbled her back a step. Cat dug her toes deep in the sand. She glanced again at Chicken, who held Lily's hand like it was the most normal thing in the world. Cat wanted to flop down and cry, like Chicken had at the airport. The difference was, Chicken knew someone would carry him and Cat didn't. She always picked herself up. She would have to figure out how to do that here.

7

During the heat of the afternoon, Lily and Chicken played Go Fish. Cat read in her room.

When she came downstairs, the house was quiet. Lily and Chicken were gone. Maybe they'd gone outside. Of course, she hadn't seen Macon since morning.

Cat pushed the sliding glass door, and as she did, a scream came from the beach. She froze for an instant. *Chicken.*

She imagined the worst—he was upset and ran down the beach. Or worse, into the waves. Her heart flip-flopped at the thought. She ran onto the sand. Chicken and Lily were there, on the beach. Somehow, Chicken had convinced her to take the laundry basket outside.

"Are you all right?" she asked when she got close enough. "I thought I heard you scream."

Chicken turned to her. "We dug up a half-eaten crab. It was super gross."

Lily smiled. "We threw it in the sand over there a ways if you want to see before a gull snatches it."

Cat would wait for her heart to return to normal before she went looking for something disgusting.

They were building a sand castle. Lily sat in the sand, but Chicken kneeled in the basket and reached over the edge to dig. He'd leaned so far, it looked like he might topple out.

"Careful of your treasures," said Lily.

He squinted up at Cat. "See my collection?"

Inside the basket were dozens of shells.

"Very nice," said Cat. She sank to the ground and scooped a handful of sand.

"When we're done, we'll fill that bucket and make the moat," Chicken explained.

Lily beamed at him. "To keep dragons out?"

Chicken looked at Lily like she'd lost her mind. "It's so sharks can live there."

He shook his head and went back to his digging, muttering "dragons" under his breath.

Cat smiled to herself, excavating a handful of sand. Moats were *obviously* for sharks. Lily hadn't totally figured out Chicken yet.

Lily handed her a plastic shovel. The shovel was flimsy, but better than using her hands.

"We'll find better toys," said Lily. "We weren't prepared."

Cat didn't want Lily making a big deal out of their visit. They would leave in three weeks, probably never come back. "Don't bother buying anything new. We won't be here long."

They worked quietly for a while. Lily mounded damp sand on the castle. After a while, Chicken said he was tired of digging. He arranged the shell collection into smaller piles.

Digging made Cat feel peaceful and calm. "Rishi's family used to take us to the beach sometimes when Mom worked."

"Sounds nice," said Lily.

"Most of the time, the water was too cold to swim," Cat went on. "But we could dig."

From the laundry basket came a *blub-blub-blub* . . . *vrooom*. Chicken was making motorboat noises. Cat and Lily flashed a quiet smile at each other.

"This is my favorite time of the day." Lily's voice was barely louder than the sound of the waves.

"The way it cools off before sunset . . . the light is so beautiful, everything glows."

Cat squeezed a mound of sand. She opened her fingers slowly. The sand had ridges from the spaces between her fingers. "My dad always talked about the light like that."

Lily paused mid-scoop. "He saw such beauty in the everyday."

Cat, startled, looked up from her hands. "Did you know him?"

"Oh, yes," said Lily. "Amanda brought him home many times, even before they were dating. He liked the island. And I loved having them here."

This seemed like a clue—one that had popped up out of nowhere. To hide her surprise, Cat concentrated on smoothing the walls of the moat. She didn't know that Macon and Lily had ever met Daddy, but they had. It sounded as if Lily liked him, even. Cat wondered what Macon thought. It would be close to impossible to find out with the way he hid in his workshop all the time. The one time he actually talked to them, he rushed off abruptly. Maybe he was the reason Mom left.

Lily squinted at something behind Cat.

"Oh, dear," she said. "Those boys shouldn't be on the dunes. They know better."

Up by the houses, three boys jumped and rolled on the sandy hills.

"The signs say 'Stay off,'" said Cat.

"The dunes are protected," said Lily. "If the beach grass dies, it will destroy the dune."

"How obnoxious," said Cat.

Lily looked like she was thinking about saying something to the boys, but instead she turned to Cat. "It's so nice having you here, Cat. You're such a great kid."

"Oh," said Cat, looking down. She squeezed the sand between her fingers. "Thanks."

"I see how you look out for Chicken," said Lily. "You do so much for him."

Cat shrugged. Chicken made speedboat noises.

"Holding a family together is a quiet kind of work," Lily continued. "Sometimes that work doesn't get noticed so much."

Cat brushed the sand from her hands, thinking. Both Mom and Chicken would go in a hundred different directions without Cat there to steady them. But sometimes it was like they didn't notice she was there. Lily had a point.

Suddenly, the boat noises stopped. Chicken peeped over the edge of the laundry basket.

"I have to poop," he announced. "Emergency."

Lily touched her hand lightly to her chest. "Gracious." She gave Chicken her hand. They hurried inside.

Cat held the basket and gathered the toys. She didn't want to build a castle anymore. The beach was deserted except for the boys playing on the dunes. They climbed to the top and flipped forward, turning a circle in the air before landing. A wheelbarrow stood at the bottom and they nearly crashed into it several times. They didn't seem to care, just clambered up the hill again, not noticing the plants they trampled. Cat inched closer.

Two boys had brown hair, and one had floppy blond hair. The blond kid was smaller than the other two. She guessed he was eight or nine—somewhere between her and Chicken in age. He wasn't as solid as the other boys, not as strong.

The biggest boy took the most daring flips. He also assigned scores to each of them according to some made-up scoring pattern. "Tanner, that's fifty points. John Harvey, that's six for you."

Cat rolled her eyes. Six points for the little blond kid when the other one got fifty? It made her sure the bigger boy was John Harvey's brother.

John Harvey frowned. "That's not fair, Briggs." His voice was surprisingly deep and raspy for a little kid.

Briggs sneered. "Don't be such a baby. You'd get more points if you managed a halfway decent flip."

John Harvey's neck flushed. He scrambled up the dune and stood at the top, waving his arms. "I'll do a backflip!"

Briggs and the other boy laughed.

"I'd love to see you try," said Briggs.

John Harvey glared at them. "A hundred points if I make it."

He threw himself backward from the top of the hill. His start was strong and at first, it seemed he would land on his feet, but he lost momentum partway. He smacked the ground face-first in the world's sandiest belly flop.

John Harvey lay still, facedown, while the other boys hooted. Briggs kicked an arc of sand across John Harvey's legs. He didn't react. Cat set down the laundry basket and moved closer. She couldn't walk away with him lying there. He could have hurt his back or neck. The bigger boys jostled each other, laughing.

"Hey," Cat said. They didn't stop. She walked closer.
"Hey!"

This time they heard her. The older boys turned her way,
and as they did, John Harvey stirred. He sat up, scrubbing at
his eyes and mouth. The sand coating his face made him look
like a sugar doughnut.

"What do *you* want?" Briggs asked.

He glared at her like she was the one who'd done something wrong. Cat couldn't stand kids who had to be so nasty.

She tilted her head at John Harvey. He looked small sitting on the ground. "Are you okay?"

Briggs and the other boy laughed. Cat frowned. That was
not the reaction she was expecting.

Briggs pushed John Harvey's shoulder. "You got a girl
standing up for you!"

Cat glared at Briggs. She didn't know what being a girl
had to do with anything. "You shouldn't pick on little kids!"

At this, the older boys started laughing so hard, they bent
over.

John Harvey's ears flamed red. He got to his feet and
stood straight. "I'm not little. I'm twelve."

Cat raised her eyebrows. Twelve? She looked at him carefully. He was short, but compact and strong-looking in a
way most little kids weren't, his face pinched in a snarl.

"What a baby," Briggs said, stretching out his voice so the
vowels took forever and a day. "What a sweet widdle baby."

"Maybe she can help you do your flip next time," added

Tanner. He grinned when this comment sent Briggs into a new wave of laughter.

Cat's face warmed, partly for herself and partly for John Harvey. "You shouldn't have been up on the dunes anyway!"

The boys straightened up. Briggs's laugh was gone and he had that sneer again.

"What do you know about it?" he asked. "Here on vacation and you're some kind of expert? Let me guess, one-week rental?"

Cat glared back at him, heart buzzing like a trapped insect. She wasn't wrong. Lily said being on the dunes was wrong, even illegal. He had no right to make her feel like she didn't belong. She straightened her shoulders.

"For your information," she began, "I am not on vacation. I am staying with my grandparents who live here." She pointed to the sign behind them. "And anyway, I don't have to be from here to know how to read. Unless you guys haven't learned how."

"Shut up," said John Harvey. He shook his hair out of his eyes. "At least we don't take a laundry basket to the beach."

Cat was about to ask what that meant coming from a kid who'd brought a wheelbarrow, but Briggs was too quick for her. With a few long steps, he crossed to the basket on the sand, scooped it with one hand, and tossed it to Tanner. Toys and seashells spilled out.

Cat clenched her fists by her sides. "Give it back. That's my brother's."

The boy tossed the basket to John Harvey in a lopsided arc. He caught it and looked toward Briggs, who jerked his head toward the dune.

John Harvey's mouth curled in a mean smile. He scaled the dune and placed the basket at the top. "Why do you have this out here anyway? Doing your laundry?" The other boys laughed.

"Why do you have that wheelbarrow?" Cat asked. "Doing some gardening?"

They ignored her.

"Let's get out of here," said Briggs. "I hate this part of the beach anyway."

She couldn't believe they were leaving Chicken's basket on the dune.

"You better go get it," Cat yelled after them.

Briggs spun around, walking backward as he shouted back at her. "Or what?"

Cat didn't have an answer.

John Harvey sneered. "Next time, we'll toss it in the ocean."

The three of them laughed and continued walking down the beach, John Harvey pushing their dumb wheelbarrow, which made stupid lines in the sand. She pushed her fingers against her eyes. She was not going to cry over a bunch of nasty, dumb island kids. She had to get the basket.

The dune was steeper than she realized. She wanted to climb it in a dash, but instead she lumbered awkwardly. If she paused to take a breath, she slid backward and stumbled on the loose sand. Finally, she found footholds and made her way to the top.

A window in the nearby house whooshed up. A balding man leaned out. "Hey now! Y'all need to get off that dune."

Cat held up the basket. "I was—" she started. The window slammed shut.

Inside, she boiled. She got yelled at, and the boys didn't hear a peep. She hurried down the dune and gathered the seashells and sand toys. It was a small island, but not a tiny one. If she was lucky, she could avoid those boys.

She slid open the glass door.

"My boat!" said Chicken.

Chicken had no idea what she'd been through to get that dumb basket, but he still could have said "thank you" for bringing it in.

"Nice to see you, too," said Cat.

Chicken shrugged. "I am glad to see you, Cat. But I am extra super glad to see my boat!" He put the basket over his head and marched around the living room.

Lily was busy chopping vegetables. Cat didn't want to talk to her anyway, not about this. She felt deflated, emptied out, after what had happened on the beach.

She turned to Chicken. "Let's see if Mom can video chat."

"Yes! I want to show her my boat."

Cat ran upstairs for her tablet and brought it back down. It took a while to connect.

"Now don't yell and don't put your face too close to the screen," she reminded Chicken.

"I won't," he said.

"Well, you always do," said Cat.

"Not *always*," said Chicken, leaning backward so far, he almost fell over.

Finally, it connected with a *ping*.

"Hey kids!" said Mom. "How are you doing? My phone is low on charge, so I can't talk for long."

"We were on the beach two times today," said Chicken. "Also we saw Macon's boat, which goes in a jar."

"Not a jar, a bottle," said Cat.

"That's nice," said Mom. "What else?"

"Lily showed us their Big Blue Book," said Chicken. "Except it's not blue, but other than that it is like our Big Blue Book."

"I saw your photos," said Cat.

Even on a tiny screen from four hundred miles away, it was easy to see that Mom was uncomfortable. "Pretty boring, right?"

Cat didn't know what she was talking about. Mom and Macon had been grinning in all those photos. That wasn't boring, that was special. The kind of special she wanted with Mom.

"You went fishing with Macon all the time," she said.

"It was a lifetime ago," Mom answered.

"Could we go this weekend when you visit?" asked Cat. "You could teach me."

"Um . . ."

"Come on, Mom, please?"

Mom sighed. "Okay. We'll see."

Cat grinned. They would fish together, be a team together. It wasn't as good as their Atlanta trip would have been, but it could be a kind of second place vacation.

"My phone is running out, let's talk later this week. Love you guys! Be good!"

"Yes, Mama," said Chicken.

"Love you, too," said Cat.

The picture cut out. Cat looked at the blank screen for a moment before turning it off. She didn't know why Mom had to be so mysterious about her past. Cat thought about everything she had learned so far—that Mom had loved fishing, that Macon was a busy doctor, that Mom had left and never come back. Nothing added up. It felt like Cat had a handful of puzzle pieces but couldn't see the picture they made.

Mom held all the pieces, but she wasn't helpful. She avoided talking about the island as much as she could. To get the answers she needed, Cat would have to be creative. If Mom wouldn't tell her, she'd have to find someone who could.

8

The sky was pink from the rising sun, and Cat wanted to watch from the deck. She wrapped herself in a fuzzy blanket and went downstairs.

The living room was dim and quiet, except for the gurgling of the coffeepot. No one was in the kitchen. She was about to push open the sliding glass door when she heard a voice behind her.

"Mornin'."

Cat turned. It was Macon. He was pouring coffee into his travel mug.

"Hey," she said. "Is it time for your walk?"

"Yes, ma'am," said Macon, tightening the lid. "This morning and every morning."

Cat wondered if the sunrise was even prettier up close to the waves. "Can I go with you?"

As soon as the words were out, she regretted them. Yesterday, Macon barely spoke three sentences before he bolted out the door. He wouldn't want her on his special morning walk.

Macon seemed surprised. "If you like. Not much to see this early in the morning, mind you."

"That's okay," she said.

Macon hesitated, but then nodded once. "There's a chill; best get yourself a sweater."

She ran for her hoodie. When she returned, he was waiting on the deck. His strides were long, and Cat had to add a half jog to her step so she wouldn't fall behind.

After a while, Cat adjusted to his speed and they reached a steady pace.

"Lily said these were turtle walks," Cat said. "Will we see any?"

Macon waved his hand toward the water. "Unlikely. We might see tracks from when they lay their eggs in the sand."

That was interesting. "How many eggs in a nest?"

"Up to sixty," Macon said. "Takes a couple of months to hatch. You and your brother will be long gone by then."

Cat looked at him sideways. She and Chicken had just arrived, but he was thinking ahead to when they'd be gone—maybe even looking forward to it. She tried again.

"That ship in the bottle was cool," she said.

"Hobbies are good," he said.

A seagull raced along the shore. "Do you do other stuff—besides the ships?"

"A bit of woodworking here and there, and I like to tinker in my shop. Used to be hard to find time for everything I wanted to do. Now I've got plenty of time to fill."

The line of trophies on the bookshelf popped into Cat's head. "What about fishing?"

He frowned a crease in the center of his forehead. "That was a long time ago."

"Mom said she'd teach me." Cat didn't say she'd had to push Mom to agree.

He sipped his coffee.

Cat remembered how upset he'd been yesterday when they talked about fishing. Maybe he was sad because he was missing all those good times with Mom. From the look of the pictures, fishing had been special for them. And he said he needed hobbies.

"You should come with us," she said.

Macon coughed. "I don't think that's a good idea."

"Why?" Cat asked. She walked five steps before she realized he wasn't beside her anymore. He stood behind her, looking out at the water. She watched him, and then walked back to where he stood. He didn't seem to be looking at anything in particular.

Cat waited.

Finally, as if nothing unusual had happened, he started walking again.

"I'd be in the way," he said, finally. "Besides, I don't like it much anymore."

Macon was as stubborn as Mom, but Cat was sure that if he tried fishing again, he would like it. Mom and Macon would have to remember all the good times they had.

"Please come, Macon," she said. "It will be fun."

"No," he snapped. "I can't. Let's turn back." He pivoted and walked back the way they came.

Cat frowned. The list of what Macon didn't like included boat rides, fishing trips, Chicken, and Cat. The list of what he liked: sea turtles and hot coffee. Seeing as Cat was neither, there was no point in trying to talk to him. On the way back she didn't bother trying to catch up.

9

The afternoon sky puffed with clouds. Macon brought down an old kite from the attic and, after much encouragement from Lily, he agreed to join them on the beach. Chicken about burst from excitement. He asked technical questions about the kite and soon he and Macon were deep in conversation about aerodynamics. They talked like they had known each other forever.

Cat pushed her toes in the sand in irritation. She guessed she could remove Chicken from the list of what Macon didn't like.

"I feel like walking," Lily said. "Come with me, Cat?"

Cat nodded at her brother. "I have to stay with him."

"We'll stay close by," said Lily.

Cat studied them. Macon was Chicken's new best friend. And Cat wouldn't go far.

Together Cat and Lily walked along the water. Cat's favorite beach find was sea glass. It was difficult to spot, so each piece felt like a treasure. So far Cat had two brown and one clear in her collection. Lily also loved the glass. She collected green and blue pieces in a big bowl on the coffee table.

Lily was explaining the way waves tumble and smooth the glass when Cat saw something out of the corner of her eye.

Macon looked at the kite in the sky. He talked and gestured but didn't realize Chicken had turned toward the water and taken a few steps toward it. A wave approached and its edge rushed over Chicken's feet. Cat thought he'd panic, but he smiled. She smiled, too, remembering how it felt to realize an ocean could be warm.

For an instant, he stood completely still.

"Warm water!" he shouted.

Macon looked at him, startled. Cat looked at Chicken hard, her brain calculating how long it would take to reach him.

He charged into the water, but stumbled. A wave went over his head and he disappeared.

"Chicken! Chicken!"

She raced across the sand, Lily right behind her. Macon was thigh-deep in the waves. He fished Chicken out of the water. When Chicken's head popped up, he looked surprised, but he was even more surprised when Macon scooped him up and held him like a baby.

Lily ran right into the water after them. "Is he all right? Is he breathing?"

Chicken answered this by throwing his head back and howling. He yelled so hard, he blocked out the sound of the waves. Macon held Chicken as he walked onto the sand. Chicken was twisting desperately in Macon's arms.

Lily patted at Chicken like she was trying to check that he was all in one piece. "Is he hurt?"

Lily didn't understand. Chicken's body was okay. But his insides were crashing harder than the waves. Macon and Lily meant well, but they were doing everything wrong.

Chicken hadn't stopped howling. He arched his back, arms pinwheeling.

Cat took a step toward them. "You're holding him too tight, Macon. And he doesn't like being on his back like that, he doesn't feel safe."

Macon didn't seem to hear. He and Lily kept fussing over Chicken. All three of them were soaking wet.

Chicken shuddered a deep breath. "Want shark."

Lily's eyebrows bunched in concern. "Macon, he wants his shark! I think it's on the kitchen counter."

"Please," Chicken sobbed. "Let me down."

"No, sir!" Macon said, still holding him. "We can't have you running in the water."

Chicken kicked at Macon, who only gripped him closer. Chicken hated being held so tight.

Cat reached out. "Give him to me."

Macon hesitated. "He's too heavy. This is safer."

Cat's eyebrows shot up fast. He was the one who let Chicken run into the water, and he thought it wasn't safe for *his own sister* to hold him?

"You should have watched him better if you care about what's safe," she said. "You're holding him too tight! He doesn't like being on his back. I know what he needs."

Lily stepped forward. Her hair was plastered to her forehead. "Macon, give him to Cat." Her usually soft voice was lined with something strong.

Macon transferred Chicken to Cat. Cat turned and walked slowly toward the house. She had to be careful she didn't fall over because Chicken *was* heavy. That was the one thing Macon was right about.

She paused to readjust Chicken's arms, which clung to her neck in a way that made breathing difficult. He was so wet, he was harder to hold, and he was somehow heavier.

"Want a shark," Chicken repeated.

"I know you do," said Cat. She staggered, but straightened again.

"Not my *toy*. I want a real one. Cookiecutter sharks like warm water, and this ocean is warm."

"Oh, Chicken," said Cat. "You'll go in when you're big, when you've learned to swim."

He didn't argue with her this time, but she thought she heard him mutter something.

She paused to hoist him up again. "What did you say?" she asked.

"Someday I'll be big," he said.

"Yes," she said. "But not today."

She carried him the rest of the way and didn't set him down until they reached the deck. She grabbed a striped towel.

"Come here," she said. She patted him dry so he wouldn't drip. Chicken needed her in a way Macon and Lily couldn't understand. Sometimes Cat didn't understand it either. She rubbed his sandy feet.

Chicken gazed over the railing. "What are they talking about?"

Cat looked up from the towel. Macon and Lily were in deep discussion. They stood far enough away that she couldn't hear them. "Probably talking about us."

Chicken turned to her with big eyes. "Will they send us away?"

Cat studied them. Lily was talking while Macon mostly nodded.

"I don't think so," she answered. "But you can't run off like that, Chicken, especially in the water. It's dangerous."

"Okay," said Chicken.

She looked at him. He was surprisingly calm for how upset he had been a few moments ago. She needed to make sure he understood how important this was.

"Promise me," she said.

"I promise," he said. "No ocean until I'm big."

The towel had done all it could do, so Cat spread it out on the deck railing to dry. "Let's find some dry clothes."

Upstairs, Chicken changed and brought his wet clothes to Cat.

"Read to me?" he asked. He held *The Broken Cookie*, which came out earlier that year.

"Sure," said Cat. They climbed onto the window seat and he stretched out next to her. The first few pages were all about Cat and Chicken at the bakery, choosing their cookies. But when they walked outside, Chicken tripped on the sidewalk. His cookie broke. Chicken stomped around the page, angry and crying.

You have a puzzle cookie!

The ending was supposed to be happy, but something about it made Cat stop short. Couldn't Caterpillar have given Chicken the *idea* for a puzzle cookie without breaking her own? Cat felt herself getting upset. On one hand, it was a story about cookies. On the other hand, it was much more.

Cat was Chicken's big sister. She would never complain when Chicken needed her. And sometimes, he did need her. Even though he was safe beside her, it made her shiver to remember his head disappearing under the wave. That was terrible, an emergency.

But a broken cookie was not an emergency. It was a little sad, and that's all.

And Caterpillar broke her cookie when she didn't have to! She made things worse for herself on purpose. It didn't seem right.

"Chicken," she said. "Why do you think book-Caterpillar solved the problem that way?"

Chicken twirled his fingers. "Because puzzle cookies are funny."

"Okay," Cat said. "But Caterpillar could have explained without breaking hers."

Chicken frowned. "All she wants is for Chicken to be happy. She doesn't care about the cookie."

Cat snapped the book shut. "She should care!"

Chicken crossed his arms. "Well, she doesn't."

"The cookie isn't the point. It's a *symbol*. The cookie represents all the things Caterpillar gives up to keep Chicken happy." Cat thought back to the last day of school, when she said no to the Toy Boat with Poppy Zhang. Chicken didn't know half of what Cat did to make him happy.

Chicken shook his head. "That's dumb. Symbols are dumb."

"Sometimes stories are more than the words on the page," said Cat.

Chicken grabbed the book from her. "That is *dumb*. If Mama wanted the story to mean something different, she would write it like that. She wouldn't be tricky."

He didn't understand. Cat shook her head in frustration. She heard a light tapping. It was Lily, in the doorway.

"Would either of you like some lemonade?" Lily asked.

"Yes," said Chicken. He hopped off the window seat and walked out, not looking back.

"Cat?"

"No, thanks," said Cat. When she heard their feet on the stairs, she shut the door. She needed time by herself.

In the window seat, she made a pillow nest. Arguing with Chicken was pointless. He didn't understand that a book could be more than one thing. On one level, it was a story about a cookie. But on a deeper level, there was so much more. Caterpillar put herself last all the time, even when she didn't have to. Cat wasn't like that. Was she?

Chicken needed so much. He needed someone to watch him, think about him constantly, and keep him safe. To remind him that going into the ocean fully clothed is a bad idea, especially for someone who can't swim. Sometimes it seemed like Chicken needed more than what Cat and Mom could give. He needed more than the two of them—he needed a crowd.

Cat didn't need a crowd, but she needed someone. She checked the time. Mom would be teaching, but she could email Rishi.

Rishi,

How's your grandma doing? I am sorry she had a stroke. I hope she is okay.

What is India like?

We're in North Carolina with my mom's parents. Weird, right? I had never met them until this week. Lily is nice. Macon is okay, I guess.

Chicken took off running into the ocean today. (He's fine.) I haven't even had a chance to tell you how he ran away on Clement Street before we left San Francisco. He scares me sometimes.

Write me or video chat when you can.

Cat

That night, Chicken fell asleep quickly, but Cat was awake. She curled up in the window seat and read. She was about to turn out the lights when she heard Macon and Lily on the deck below. They sat in the porch swing, which *crick*ed over the sound of the waves. Listening was probably not the right thing to do, but she couldn't help it.

"Never been so scared—" Macon's voice rose up.

"It ended up all right—" said Lily, soothing.

"Shouldn't have turned my back, but he was so interested in the kite—"

"You didn't do anything wrong. He got distracted, that's all."

Macon said something back that sounded like: "Don't know if I have it in me."

Their voices were low. Cat leaned toward the window, straining her ears.

"It's like dynamite," said Macon finally. "I could mess it up and they could go away. It would be all my fault." The words were choppy, like it hurt to say them.

Lily answered, but her voice was quiet. The porch swing *crick*ed five hundred times before Cat crawled under the covers next to her brother, and it was still *crick*ing when she closed her eyes and fell asleep.

10

The morning sun woke Cat. Chicken was snoring, and Cat couldn't get back to sleep. She put on her sweatshirt and went downstairs. She didn't expect to be invited on a walk, not after yesterday. But there were two mugs on the counter.

"Morning," Macon said. "All ready to go?"

It was like they'd already decided that they'd walk together. She nodded.

He picked up the blue mug and nodded at the silver. "That's yours."

Cat looked at the silver mug, surprised.

"Hot chocolate," he said. "I thought coffee might stunt your growth." He turned and headed to the door before she could thank him.

Outside, there was a mist that reminded her of San

Francisco fog. She balanced her mug and followed him into the morning. They walked in silence for a while, sipping their hot drinks. Cat's was creamy and delicious.

Cat squeezed the wet sand with her toes. She wanted to ask Macon more about his morning walks. "So, what made you start looking for the turtles?"

Macon kept walking his fast walk. "I like them. Most of the time they know exactly what they are doing. It's only when people get in their way that there are problems."

"What do you mean get in their way?"

"Like your grandmother said, the lights confuse them. Sometimes they get sick from eating trash, especially balloons and plastic. I clean up as I walk."

"That's a nice thing to do."

"Not a big deal, really. Just being there when I can."

A few steps from the water lay shards of a purple sand shovel. She bent to gather them.

"Half of life is showing up," Macon said quietly, almost to himself. "And some things are worth showing up for."

They didn't say anything for the rest of the walk.

Back at the house, Chicken tore into a stack of pancakes. Macon and Cat took turns washing their hands.

"Caterpillar," said Chicken, "Lily told me about the library reading program. If you sign up, you get prizes! I am going to read every book they have about sharks."

"But you probably won't earn many prizes," said Cat. "Remember, we won't be here long." She bit into a strawberry.

Chicken streamed syrup over his half-eaten pancakes. "I will earn lots of prizes. You'll see."

Macon turned to Lily. "Are you planning to take him?"

"I'll take him," said Cat. "It's not far."

Macon cleared his throat. "After yesterday, I think you should have an adult with you."

Cat shook her head. "We're fine! We take the bus all over San Francisco. We can walk a few blocks ourselves."

Lily looked at Cat, and then she looked at Macon.

"Chicken, get your shoes," said Cat.

He galloped to the living room. Macon cleared the breakfast dishes. He spoke to Lily in a low voice, frowning.

"I won't get lost," said Cat. She looked at Macon's back. She wanted him to remember yesterday's mistake. "And I know how to keep him safe."

Macon stood at the sink, not facing her.

"Go on," said Lily. "Have fun."

Macon didn't say a word.

"Fine," said Cat. "Bye." She and Chicken left. Cat let the door close hard behind her.

On the sidewalk, Chicken had a question. "Is Macon mad at us?"

Cat was still irritated. "Of course not," said Cat sharply. "But he thinks I'm a little kid like you."

Chicken frowned. "Are you mad?"

"No!" said Cat. "But he should see I'm not a baby."

"I'm not a baby either," said Chicken firmly.

Cat gave him a shoulder squeeze. "I know."

The town was quiet. There were a few souvenir shops, a general store, and an ice cream place called Miss Sunshine's. A square playground was surrounded by big trees.

"Playground!" said Chicken.

"Library first," said Cat.

Outside the library were statues of sea creatures, including giant sea turtles and sharks. Kids climbed and jumped on them. Chicken gazed at them longingly.

"Later," said Cat. "We'll play after."

He nodded and they climbed the steps. A sign said Summer Reading Program Kickoff Today. Inside, kids were everywhere.

Someone tapped them on the shoulder. It was a woman with white makeup on her face, a purple wig, and a giant red painted-on grin.

"Aaaaaaah!" said Chicken, hiding behind Cat.

The clown sighed.

"Sorry," said Cat.

"I've been getting that a lot today." The clown pointed. "Registration for the summer reading program is thataway."

"Thanks," said Cat. They went through the glass doors to a room with walls full of murals and tall windows. Shelves were dotted with handwritten librarian recommendations. Throughout the room were displays on different summer-related topics. Chicken gasped when he saw a papier-mâché hammerhead topping an arrangement of shark books.

"I want them all!" he said.

"Let's get three. Only three."

Chicken had already stacked a dozen in his arms. When Cat raised her eyebrows he said, "I know, I know. I'm *browsing*."

"We'll sign up and then you can look all you want."

They gave their names to the librarian behind the desk, who wrote down their information in a big book. She handed them each a paper sea turtle with their names.

Chicken traced his finger along the list of prizes. "I want the mini golf!"

"You want to *go* mini golfing."

"Nope," said Chicken. "It says 'Mini Golf' right here."

Cat decided not to argue. "You better get reading if you want anything." They found a table by the bulletin board and a bearded librarian shelving books. A bright green flyer on the wall caught Cat's eye.

Cat read the flyer again. If Rishi were here, he would enter. He would love a contest like this. Maybe she should try it. She didn't know how to fish, but Mom could teach her. That wasn't a bad idea at all. She reread the form.

She turned to the librarian. "Excuse me, do you know where I can find the entry for the contest?"

GINGERBREAD ISLAND YOUTH FISHING CONTEST

FUN ★ PRIZES

Kids ages 8-14! Catch all the fish you can between 5:00 a.m. and 8:00 p.m. on the Gingerbread Island Fishing Pier Saturday, July 9. This year's cash prize sponsored by Small Fry Food Truck. Enter at Willis General Store by June 25.

The librarian looked up. "Should be right by the bulletin board. We must have run out."

"Okay," said Cat. It was a silly idea anyway.

"Let me see if we have any behind the desk. If not, they should have them over at Willis General."

The librarian went to check and Cat turned back to the board. It didn't say how big the cash prize might be. Could it be enough to buy an airplane ticket to visit Rishi later this summer?

Suddenly she heard a wail behind her. She froze. She turned, expecting to see Chicken's face full of tears.

But instead it was a small boy with dark brown hair and freckles polka-dotting every inch of his pale skin. His face was streaked with blood. He gripped a book but Chicken's hands were tugging it from his grasp.

As Cat watched, the flow of blood became a small river, making rusty spots on the boy's shirt.

Cat crossed to them quickly. "Let go of that book," she said to Chicken. Startled, he took a step back.

The boy clung to the book, which now had blood spots on it, too. Cat grimaced.

She bent down to be at his eye level. "Hey," she said. "Are you okay? Are you here with your mom or anyone?"

He shook his head and wailed again.

"It's okay," Cat tried again. "We'll help you."

The boy sobbed. Chicken was quiet.

Cat touched his arm. "Did you hurt him, Chicken?"

Chicken nodded.

Cat gasped. She couldn't believe it. "You hurt this little boy?"

Chicken nodded again, his eyes filling with tears.

The boy said, "Harriet!" Cat turned to see a girl coming around the corner. She was about Cat's age, with the same dark hair and freckles as the little boy.

"Neddie," she said. "What happened?"

Neddie cried and pointed at Chicken. Harriet frowned at Chicken and Cat.

"I'm so sorry," said Cat. "He would never hurt anyone."

Harriet looked up from her brother. "Well, obviously that's not true."

"On purpose I mean," Cat said.

Harriet arched her eyebrows. "There's a first time for everything, I guess."

Chicken's eyes shimmered.

"Does anyone have a tissue?" Harriet asked.

The bearded librarian came back. He held an ice pack and a handful of scratchy paper towels. "Hi there, Neddie, looks like you've got yourself a big old nose bleed."

Neddie took the wad of paper towels and pressed it to his nose.

It was clear that the librarian knew these kids. No one knew Cat and Chicken.

"I'm sorry," Cat said softly. "We're really sorry." Everyone was looking at the boy.

Harriet scrunched a fresh paper towel to his nose. "Pinch it, Neddie."

They had to get out of there. "Come on, Chicken," Cat whispered.

"My books," he whispered back.

He didn't get it. It wasn't okay to smack this Neddie kid in the face and then collect his books like nothing had happened. She grabbed his shoulder. "Forget the books—we have to go!"

Cat forced him to walk quickly. They dodged the clown in the lobby, then went outside.

"Can we play?" asked Chicken.

"No!" said Cat. "Not after what you did."

They walked back to the house and stood at the bottom of the stairs. She had to make him understand that he'd done something wrong.

"Hurting people is bad," said Cat.

Chicken's eyes filled with tears. "I'm not bad."

"I didn't say you were bad. But hurting people is bad. It is, Chicken."

Chicken wiped his eyes.

"If you tell Macon and Lily they won't let us go anywhere by ourselves. We'll be trapped here."

Chicken thought it over. "I won't tell if you promise to take me to the park tomorrow."

Cat's eyes popped. "Are you blackmailing me?"

"I'm making a deal," he said evenly.

She didn't see much choice. The idea of explaining to Macon and Lily made her head hurt. Besides, she didn't mind going to the park. She nodded.

Chicken hurried up the stairs and swung the door wide. "Lily, I'm back!"

Chicken had surprised her. First he fought at the library, when Chicken never hurt anyone. Then he used the fight to bargain for a park trip. She'd underestimated her brother. His marshmallow heart had grown a row of teeth.

That afternoon, Chicken wanted to play sharks with Lily in the guest room. Lily was Chicken's new best friend. When they had returned without books, she promised to take Chicken again later in the week. This was fine with Cat, who had crossed the library off her list. She never wanted to see Harriet and Neddie again.

Macon was sweeping the kitchen floor. Cat didn't want to talk to him, so she decided to video chat Mom.

When it connected, Mom smiled big.

"Hey, Cat!"

"Hey, Mom," said Cat. "Are you having a good day?"

"Fantastic!" said Mom. She launched into a story about how inspired she was by her talented students.

Cat smiled and nodded in all the right places. But the more Mom talked about how excited she was, the more Cat realized how unfun life on the island was.

Mom wrapped up her story and gazed at Cat.

"Is the island too boring for you?" Mom asked.

The *scritch* of Macon's broom paused for a minute. Cat glanced up to see if he was listening, but he had only stopped to retrieve the dustpan.

She was glad Mom could tell something was wrong, but she didn't want to say much with Macon there. "Boring isn't the problem."

"Have you found some nice kids?"

"I found some kids," she said. "But no *nice* ones."

"Island kids can be close-knit," said Mom.

"Yeah. And there is one boy who is straight-up awful, and

there is a girl who—" Cat didn't want to explain Chicken's fight. "She wasn't nice either."

Mom listened. Sometimes she was so wrapped up in her work, she couldn't see anything past her nose. Other times, she knew when to let Cat talk.

"Are you that unhappy?" Mom asked.

Cat *was* unhappy, but talking wouldn't help. "It will be okay. It's just three weeks anyway."

"That's my girl. Listen, I need to run, but I will see you this weekend, okay?"

Cat nodded. "Hey, Mom? I love you."

"I love you, too."

They clicked off. Cat's face was reflected in the blank screen. The door closed, and Cat realized Macon had left without saying good-bye. Typical.

Rishi,

The kids here are a disaster. Chicken gave a kid at the library a nosebleed. That is all the breaking news for now. I'll let you know if we get in any other brawls.

Cat

P.S. I may (may!) learn how to fish. Turns out my mom is some kind of expert fisherperson, if you can believe that. She's going to teach me. How did you learn? Do you have any tips?

11

That morning when Cat came downstairs, Macon was halfway out the kitchen door.

"Are you leaving already?" Cat asked.

He paused in the doorframe. "No," he started. He cleared his throat. "I'm not going today, actually. I have another project."

His voice sounded funny. Cat looked at the sky to see if a storm was coming, but it was clear. The sun peeked over the horizon, sharing its pinkish light with the water and sand.

So it wasn't the weather. Besides, Lily said he never missed his walks, rain or shine. A sharp thought grew inside her. It wasn't that he wanted to skip his walk. He didn't want to walk with *her*.

"Oh," Cat said. "I didn't really want to go anyway."

That was a lie. But she didn't want him to know she cared.

She sat on the sofa and picked up her book. She wouldn't look at him, but she could peek from the corner of her eye.

Macon nodded to the counter, where Cat's mug stood alone. "I made your hot chocolate."

If he thought that was going to make things okay, he was wrong.

Cat shrugged. "Thanks," she said crisply.

Macon hesitated, but Cat kept her eyes on her book.

"It's there if you change your mind." He closed the door with a click. Cat closed her book and looked at the waves.

When Cat was in first grade, she got her first paper cut. She finished her math worksheet early, and, out of boredom, ran her hand down the paper's edge. She did it a few times before slicing herself right in the tender part between thumb and forefinger. It hurt, but the surprise of it was worse. She hadn't realized paper could hurt.

That's how it felt when Macon cancelled the turtle walk. Without her realizing it, the walks had become special. She thought of Macon's long strides in the sand and how he'd stop suddenly to look out at the water, sipping from his mug. Some people filled up space with all their words, but Macon wasn't like that. He was careful, like each word meant something. Cat thought they were alike in that way.

Even if her feelings were hurt, she shouldn't let hot chocolate go to waste. She drank it and watched the sun rise higher, until she heard someone hopping down the stairs.

Chicken skipped the bottom two steps with a crash. Lily padded behind him.

"I can't wait for the park!" he announced.

"Breakfast first." Lily poured a bowl of cereal and slid it across the counter. "Is this something the two of you would like to do together? Or should I come along?"

Cat wasn't going to get in the habit of counting on Lily, because probably the minute Cat got used to her, Lily would cut it off, like Macon had done.

"I think we'll go by ourselves," said Cat. "It's how we're used to doing things."

Lily's eyes flickered for a minute, and then she nodded. "Another day, then." She turned to put the milk back in the fridge.

Cat hadn't meant to hurt Lily's feelings. But she was all twisted up inside from Macon. Besides, she and Chicken managed best when they were on their own. She turned to her brother. "Ready?"

They took the stairs double, clomping as loud as Macon did. They took the sidewalk to the park. When they got there, Chicken pushed past the open gate, heading for the swings. Cat hadn't expected to recognize any faces, but Neddie twirled on the metal merry-go-round, laughing like yesterday's bloody nose had never happened.

Cat turned and saw Neddie's sister sitting under a tree. Harriet. She had a book in her lap, but she was looking at Cat.

Cat wasn't sure what to do. Maybe she could pretend she hadn't seen Harriet.

But then, Harriet closed her book. "Hey."

"Hey," said Cat.

"You're not from here," said the girl. Up close, she was even more freckly than her brother. Her brown hair was tight in a ponytail worn low on her head and her shirt had a rainbow. She peered up at Cat.

"I'm Cat," said Cat. Maybe the girl didn't remember her.

"You guys left fast yesterday," said Harriet.

Cat gulped. So much for the idea of not being recognized. "I didn't know what to do. I felt really bad that Chicken hurt your brother."

Harriet tilted her head to the side. "Did you call your brother 'Chicken'?"

"Uh, yeah, everyone calls him that."

"For real? Is that his actual name?"

Cat studied Harriet's face to see if she was being nasty. The corners of her mouth were turned up, but it was friendly. Mostly, she looked curious. She even leaned toward Cat, like it would help her hear the answer faster.

"His real name is Henry, but when he was born I thought he looked like a chicken, so we called him that. It just stuck."

Harriet smiled big. "When my brother was born, he looked like a rat." Harriet squinted at the merry-go-round, where Neddie twirled in circles. "He still does, a bit, around the eyes."

Cat held in a smile. She knew from experience that it wasn't always okay to laugh at someone's brother. "Is he okay?"

Harriet closed her book. "My mom says he's got a sensitive nose. My dad says he bleeds like a stuck pig if someone looks at him sideways." She shook her head and sighed. "But either way, he's completely fine. I'm sorry I snapped at you yesterday."

"Still, Chicken shouldn't have hurt him."

Harriet frowned. "Neddie told me he grabbed Chicken's book, but Chicken wouldn't let go. When Neddie lost his grip he smacked himself in the nose with his own hand."

"Oh." When Chicken told her he hurt the boy, Cat thought she understood. She should have known Chicken wouldn't hurt someone on purpose. She should have given him a chance to explain.

"I'm glad I saw you again. Are you here on vacation?"

"Sort of," said Cat.

Harriet narrowed her eyes. "How can you be sort of on vacation?"

"We're visiting our grandparents."

"Oh! Are your grandparents Dr. Stone and Ms. Lily?"

Cat nodded. "Yep."

"I heard you were visiting. We live around the corner. Your grandma is nice."

"She is," said Cat.

"It's not that your grandpa is bad," Harriet said. "I don't know him well. No one does. He keeps to himself, that's all."

That was one way to put it. Stubborn was another. He'd even changed his daily walk to avoid Cat. Not that she wanted to share that with Harriet.

Cat nodded. "He's pretty serious."

Harriet scooted over to make room. "You can sit here, if you want."

Cat sat against the tree, next to Harriet, and they watched their brothers play.

It turned out Harriet was ten and a half, a bit younger than Cat. She was in the middle of two brothers, six-year-old Neddie and fifteen-year-old Walt. The Kincaids lived on Gingerbread Island all year, like Macon and Lily. Mr. Kincaid was a contractor and worked on island houses. Mrs. Kincaid worked on the mainland as an accountant, but sometimes did her work from home. For school, Harriet and her brothers also crossed to the mainland.

Harriet frowned like crazy when Cat told her where she was from. It turned out that wasn't a grumpy frown: it was Harriet's thinking face.

"San Francisco? Do you ride on trolleys?"

"I've been on a cable car, but not that often. They run on the other side of the city."

"Is it foggy?"

"Not all the time. But summer is foggy and cold."

"Foggy and cold in summer? Wish we had some of that here. Summer here is HOT, if you hadn't noticed. Which reminds me, have you had ice cream yet?" She pointed to Miss Sunshine's.

"Not yet," said Cat.

"It's really good. What's your favorite flavor?"

"Mint chocolate chip. What's yours?"

"Rocky road!" said Harriet. "Although really I like everything."

"We could go there sometime," Cat said. "With our brothers, I mean."

Harriet shot her a sideways look. "Or maybe without our brothers."

Cat looked at the boys, who had moved to the sandbox. "Don't you like hanging out with Neddie?"

Harriet shrugged. "Sometimes, but not every day. Two times already this week and I'm practically at my maximum."

Cat grinned. She didn't have a limit for Chicken—he needed her too much—but it might be nice to hang out with someone her own age.

Harriet checked her watch. "We have to go. Dentist appointment. Neddie, come on!"

The boys glanced up but then returned to their digging.

"Chicken!" Cat called. "One-minute warning."

Harriet walked to the sandbox and Cat followed.

"Come on, we have to go," said Harriet.

Neddie had filled a yellow pail close to full. "I'm not ready yet."

Harriet sighed. "I think I just hit my maximum."

"Thirty-second warning," Cat told Chicken.

Neddie scooped a final handful of sand in the bucket. "Now I'm ready!"

The four walked on the sidewalk together. When they were a few houses from Macon and Lily's, Harriet broke off midsentence. "Look at that! Is it yours?"

It was at the bottom of the stairs. Lemon yellow with shiny silver handlebars, a flowered basket, and a metallic purple bicycle seat that sparkled in the sun. On the back a novelty license plate spelled Amanda.

The workshop door opened.

"Fixed it up a bit this morning," said Macon. "Was in pretty good shape actually. Tightened the bolts and removed some rust."

"Cool bike, Dr. Stone."

"Thank you, Harriet. Hello, Ned. How's your mama?"

"She's good, thanks," Harriet answered. "We better get going, Neddie. See you around, Cat."

"Bye, Harriet. Bye, Neddie," said Cat.

Chicken stomped upstairs. Cat listened for the sound of the door opening, and heard Lily say hello. He would be okay for a few minutes while she looked at the bike. She touched the license plate.

"I can take that off, if you want."

"No, that's okay. They never have 'Cat' anyway."

"They never have 'Macon' either." He smiled and Cat smiled back.

A thought occurred to her. "Wait a minute, is that why you didn't want to walk today?"

He looked at her sheepishly. "I needed just a bit more time to get it fixed up."

"Oh," said Cat, almost to herself. "I thought you didn't want to walk with me."

Macon's mouth turned down. He shook his head sadly.

"I wanted to do something nice," he said. "Somehow, I always get things wrong."

"I thought maybe I was bothering you," she said. "That's all."

"I like the company. You're welcome anytime—every time." He cleared his throat. Macon glanced away. "There's a helmet, too. I know kids wear them these days." He went back to his workshop and shut the door, leaving Cat alone with the bike.

Cat ran her hands over the handlebars, so shiny, they glowed. That morning she was certain Macon couldn't stand her, and then he went and did something so thoughtful. He said she was welcome anytime. And he gave her this beautiful bike.

Cat hopped on the seat and imagined riding down Ocean Road with a breeze on her face and Harriet by her side. First a friend, and now a bike? The summer was starting to look up.

12

The sun was barely up but already it felt warm. Puffy clouds of foam had washed on the shore. Cat held her mug and watched a pelican dive for a fish in the waves.

"Macon?" Cat asked. "Did you know there's a fishing contest coming up?"

He squinted out at the water. "That so?"

Cat kicked a patch of foam and watched it flutter to the sand. "Can I ask something?"

Macon nodded.

"What's the deal with fishing? Why do people like it so much?"

The corner of Macon's mouth popped up in a half smile. "Fish are good eating."

"Maybe." Cat was skeptical. If it was about eating fish, it

would be easier to get them from the store. "Seems like a lot of work."

"I don't know about that," Macon said. "Looking at the waves, being in nature, standing side by side with someone. The catching part is a bonus."

Cat was quiet, thinking. Supposedly, Macon didn't like fishing anymore, but that's not what his words said.

Macon continued. "You learn different things when you stand side by side with someone. You're together, focused on the same goal. Sometimes you might talk, other times not at all."

"Like our turtle walks?" asked Cat.

Macon smiled and patted her shoulder. "A lot like that."

Cat knew what to do. She should enter the contest. It would solve everything. It was exactly what everyone needed.

Macon might have tried to argue that he didn't like fishing anymore, but fishing was exactly what he needed. He talked about it like it was something special. And if Macon loved fishing and missed it after all these years, it made sense that Mom did, too. If Cat learned to fish it would bring everyone together. It was a big plan, but Cat knew she could do it. As soon as she finished breakfast, she'd ride to the general store and enter the contest.

When they returned, Lily had breakfast waiting. Chicken waved a pair of binoculars.

"I'm glad you're back," he said. "We're going to stand on

the deck and look for shark fins. And then we're going to the library to check out books."

Cat sat at the counter and began to eat. "Who is 'we'? You and Lily?"

"Me and *you*," said Chicken.

Cat frowned. "But we didn't make plans."

"You weren't here," Chicken explained. "So I made plans for us."

Cat tried to squash down her irritation. "That's not how it works. You have to *ask* before making plans with someone."

"*Fine*," said Chicken. "Will you watch sharks and go to the library with me?"

It was the kind of question that wasn't really a question. He expected her to do what he wanted without complaining. Cat wanted to say no, but hesitated. She wasn't sure it was worth a fight.

Lily stepped in. "Now, Chicken, I thought the two of us were going to the library."

Cat felt a glint of hope, but Chicken crossed his arms.

"Come here," Cat said. She leaned toward him. "We can look for sharks later, I promise. I want to ride my bike before it gets too hot."

His face softened. "Maybe we can read my library books, too."

"Definitely," said Cat.

Before she left, she said thanks to Lily. Downstairs, she

wheeled the yellow bicycle from the driveway. Harriet said her house was nearby. Cat didn't know which house exactly, but maybe she'd be lucky and Harriet or Neddie would be outside.

She pedaled slowly. The houses on Harriet's block were low to the ground, painted brightly, and had a friendly look. She spotted a purple house with a garden jammed full of plants and intricate sculptures. Seven kinds of wind chimes dangled from the awning and a pair of Neddie-size rain boots stood by the door.

Cat was making up her mind about knocking when a woman came out of the garage and wheeled a recycling bin to the curb. She had lots of freckles. When she saw Cat, she smiled widely. "Hey, are you waiting for one of my gremlins?"

Cat smiled. "I wanted to see if Harriet could ride bikes. I'm Cat."

"Hello, Cat! I'm Mrs. Kincaid. Your grandma told me you were visiting. I'll get Harriet."

Harriet came out of her house barefoot, blinking in the sun. Her hair stuck up in the back. "Hey," she said to Cat.

"Hey," Cat said back. "Want to go with me to the store?"

"To Willis General?" asked Harriet. "Let me get my shoes on." She returned in a minute holding her sneakers. She was smiling by the time she finished tying them.

"Takes me a minute to wake up, sorry about that." She went in the overstuffed garage and returned a few minutes later wheeling a red ten-speed. The bike was so tall, it didn't look like Harriet could get her leg over the seat.

"Your bike is huge," said Cat.

Harriet adjusted her helmet. "Technically, it belongs to my brother Walt."

Harriet sprinted down the driveway. Just when it seemed the bike could race down the street on its own, Harriet jumped on. She wobbled for a terrible moment, but stayed upright.

Cat pedaled to catch up. They looped around downtown and coasted past the library before Harriet veered into a narrow alley. Cat followed her. They leaned their bikes against the wall.

They walked around the corner to a glossy green door with gold letters spelling out Willis General. A bell jangled when Harriet pulled the gold doorknob.

"Hey there, Harriet," said the woman behind the counter. Her skin was dark brown and her hair was in a tortoiseshell clip.

"Hey there, Ms. Willis," said Harriet. "This is my friend Cat. Her grandparents are Dr. Stone and Ms. Lily."

"Amanda Stone's daughter?" asked the woman. "It's nice to meet you, Cat. I'm Louise Willis. My Shonda went to school with your mama. We sure do miss her around here."

Cat paused. It was weird to think of strangers missing Mom.

After a long moment, she finally remembered her manners. "Nice to meet you, too."

Ms. Willis pointed at a stack of lime-green flyers. "Are y'all going to enter the contest?"

"I think so," said Cat.

Ms. Willis beamed. "That's wonderful. Take a pencil from the jar on the counter if you need one."

Cat took a flyer. "Thanks."

The girls browsed the aisles. They could have spent days there without seeing everything. In the first three rows were taffy barrels, glass jars overflowing with a rainbow of candy, racks of seed packets, soap liquids and powders, spatulas and shiny silver tools, and a hundred different types of pens. The door jangled as people came and went. Ms. Willis's sweet voice chatted with everyone like she'd known them forever. Maybe she had.

Past the postcard rack was the counter with the box for the entry forms. Cat chose a stumpy pencil.

"My mom said to get toothpaste," said Harriet. "I'll be right back." She disappeared around an aisle.

Cat had almost finished the form when something tickled her leg. She looked down and saw the scruffiest face looking back, a small dog that apparently had been assembled from leftover dog parts. Its legs were short but its paws were huge, and it had a long body with a fluffy, wagging tail. Its coat was hairy—mostly white with brown spots. One ear stuck up and one hung down. Its tongue was way too long and hung out even though its mouth was closed. Cat reached down. The dog rolled over and let Cat rub its soft belly.

"What a good girl," whispered Cat.

"Hey! Whatcha doing with my dog!" Cat looked up quickly. The dog flipped herself to standing.

At the end of the aisle was that boy from the dunes. John Harvey, with the floppy hair. Cat straightened up.

"Stop messing with her," he said. His voice had that hoarse sound to it.

Cat frowned. "I didn't do anything!"

The boy crossed his arms. "Come here, Dixie," he called. The dog shook herself, tags jingling, but didn't budge.

"Dixie, come!" said the boy.

Dixie wagged her tail and looked at Cat with a quiet grin, tongue hanging out the side of her mouth. Clearly, she was a dog with her own opinions.

"What did you do to her?" demanded John Harvey. He said it loud enough that shoppers turned and looked at Cat.

There was movement at Cat's side. Harriet was there.

"She didn't do a thing to your dog, John Harvey Dawson. Why are you completely awful?" asked Harriet, her fist clenched around her shopping bag.

John Harvey's eyes narrowed. "What's it to you?"

"Cat's my friend," said Harriet simply.

It wasn't the time for smiling, but Cat snuck a little one anyway. She had a friend on the island. It was official.

"Why do you have that form?" he asked, nodding at the green paper in Cat's hand.

Harriet narrowed her eyes right back. "Why do you think?"

"Seriously? You're thinking of entering?" he asked. He wore the same snarl he'd had on the beach.

Cat scowled. "Not *thinking* about it. Doing it."

John Harvey's mouth dropped open for a second and then he started fake-laughing like it was the funniest thing he had ever heard, that same doubled-over laughter that the older boys on the beach had laughed at him.

"Yeah," Cat found herself saying. "And I'm going to win."

Harriet's eyebrows popped up for an instant, but she squashed them down into a normal expression. "Yeah!"

John Harvey stopped laughing. "Doubt it. I've got four years of trophies at home and they'd be right lonely without this year's. I know how to catch anything and everything."

"Well," said Cat. "Maybe you've lost your touch, seeing as you can't catch your own dog." She wheeled around and strode to the door, with Harriet close behind.

Once they were back in the alley, Cat leaned on the wall. She had to catch her breath.

"That . . . was . . . amazing!" Harriet shouted. "When you walked out like that! I would pay a million bucks to see the reaction on his dumb face."

"He's nasty," said Cat.

"He's got three brothers and each is worse than the one that came before," said Harriet. "My mom says they don't have enough eyes on them. My dad says they're trouble."

John Harvey definitely seemed like trouble. Trouble on the beach and trouble in the store. Trouble wrapped up in that sneer when he'd bragged about his trophies.

"At first I wanted to enter for fun," said Cat. "But now I want to win. He's not in charge of the contest, and he's not the boss of the island."

The door jangled open and John Harvey stomped past the alleyway. Happy little Dixie trotted behind him.

Cat turned to Harriet. "He was making that up, right? He hasn't *really* won for the last four years straight?"

"Nope," Harriet said.

Cat breathed out. Of course he hadn't won a contest all those years in a row. He was talking big to try to make someone else look small.

"That's a relief," Cat said.

"Oh," said Harriet, shaking her head. "I meant no, he wasn't making it up. He was telling the truth. He wins every year."

Cat had been puffed up from anger, but Harriet's words shrank her down to size. She'd made a big promise against a nasty kid, and she didn't even know how to fish.

"My mom will only be here on weekends. How am I going to learn enough to beat John Harvey?" Her silly fishing dream was crashing around her like the waves of the Atlantic. It would be so embarrassing if she showed up and didn't catch a single fish.

As they rode away from downtown, Cat thought about

the contest. She thought of Mom teaching her to fish, of Macon joining them. She thought of standing up to John Harvey. She was going to show him, and not in the way sweet, kind Caterpillar from the books would do. She wanted to learn everything there was about fishing so she could take that trophy from him and smile while she did it.

Harriet skidded to a stop at Macon and Lily's driveway. "I can help. I don't know how to fish, but we've got a garage full of gear."

"That sounds great," said Cat. How hard could it be?

"We should start right away so you have lots of time to practice," said Harriet. "Tonight?"

"Definitely!" said Cat.

They made a plan to meet at the pier. Harriet ran with the too-big bike, then leaped on and rode away.

Meeting in the evening was tricky because it would change Chicken's bedtime schedule. He was picky about routines. But earlier today, Lily had helped, and maybe she could help again. It was worth a try. After all, it wasn't every day Cat made a friend, gained an enemy, and entered a fishing contest.

Cat wrote out directions for Lily, filling an entire page with her small, loopy writing. She'd explained everything, including how to give Chicken back scratches. She underlined the part about double checking that he brushed his teeth.

Lily studied the paper, nodding.

Chicken pulled at the hem of her shirt. "Don't go."

No matter how much time she made for Chicken, he always wanted more. The entire afternoon they'd looked through binoculars in hopes of a shark sighting. They'd spotted several, but they were all imaginary. Chicken insisted their chances would be better if they sailed the green laundry basket into the waves. Sometimes his imagination went too far, but Cat was almost positive he'd been joking. Either way, they'd stayed dry and safe on Macon and Lily's deck.

Cat leaned down to talk to him in a whisper. "Promise I'll be back soon."

He studied her face, thinking. "Will you read an extra book tonight?"

"Of course," said Cat, hugging him. She stood at the door, hesitating. She'd triple-checked the list, but what if she had forgotten something?

"We'll manage," said Lily kindly. "Don't make Harriet wait."

Cat looked at the clock. She was going to have to hurry.

She hugged Chicken once more and then bounced out the door, down the steps, and toward the pier. Harriet was there, waiting—fishing pole in hand and a pile of gear at her feet.

"Dad says the tides are changing," said Harriet. "So it's good timing."

Cat examined the stuff. "Is this all your dad's?"

Harriet shook her head. "This is my brother Walt's stuff."

"Nice of him to let us borrow it," said Cat.

Harriet looked sheepish. "He's at camp, so he doesn't exactly know. But what he doesn't know won't hurt him." She held up a sliced hot dog in a zipper bag. "Bait."

They picked a spot in the middle of the pier. Cat pushed a chunk of hot dog on the hook, then paused. "Do I kind of fling it or what?"

Harriet scrunched her forehead. "I'm not sure."

Cat pushed the button on the handle of the reel. The line sank into the water and drifted sideways.

Harriet looked down at the water.

"Hello, girls." Both Cat and Harriet turned to see John Harvey, smirking, with Dixie at his feet. "Fishing? Or should I say *trying* to fish?"

"Don't worry yourself," said Harriet.

"How come you're everywhere we go?" asked Cat. "Are you following us?"

"It's an island, did you notice? You can expect to see the same people. That's how it works," he said. The girls ignored him. "What are you all using for bait?"

"Hot dog," said Harriet.

"Hot dog! Ocean fish don't eat hot dogs," said John Harvey.

"Oh, yeah?" said Harriet, glaring. "Cat's already caught three big ones."

John Harvey squinted disbelievingly. "None in your bucket."

"We released them," said Cat, thinking fast.

"Obviously," added Harriet.

John Harvey pointed to the end of the pier. "That's *my* lucky spot. Don't even think about horning in."

Cat rolled her eyes. He walked off, Dixie trotting behind.

"He's such a worm," said Harriet, shaking her head. "We have *got* to figure this out. Cat, do you feel anything pulling?"

Cat shook her head.

The waves whooshed below. After a few moments, John Harvey whooped.

Harriet groaned. "I can't look."

He pulled a fish over the railing, cut the line, and dropped it in his bucket.

"It's a big one!" he called over to them. The girls looked away.

Cat felt a tug on the line. She turned to Harriet excitedly. But when she reeled it in, there was no fish. And the hot dog was missing, too.

"I guess ocean fish do eat hot dogs after all," Cat said. She pushed another chunk of meat on the hook and dropped her line.

As the sky darkened, they heard John Harvey whoop again.

Harriet frowned. "He's hogging all the luck. Let's try again tomorrow."

They walked toward the houses together.

"Tomorrow my mom will come fishing with us," said Cat. "She has more trophies than even John Harvey."

"Cool," said Harriet. "She can help us."

They made plans to meet tomorrow and said good-bye at Macon and Lily's driveway. Harriet walked backward, waving, until she disappeared around the corner.

Cat was still smiling when she walked into the kitchen. Lily and Macon were having tea at the counter.

"Where's Chicken?" Cat asked.

Lily smiled proudly. "He fell asleep when I was reading to him in the guest room."

Cat hadn't expected that. He must be feeling comfortable with Lily. That seemed like a good thing. She would check on him later.

"Cat, your mom called," Lily said.

She'd probably been on the road a while. "That's great. Is she almost here?"

Lily shifted in her seat. "She wanted you to call."

Cat picked up the phone and dialed.

"Hey, honey," said Mom when she answered. "It's not going to work out for me to come this weekend."

Cat's insides sank. "What? Why?"

"The college is having a reception for me. I have to be here for it. I wouldn't have enough time to get to you and get back here."

"But I really wanted to see you." Cat *needed* Mom, couldn't she see?

"I wanted to see you, too," said Mom. "And Chicken. He cried when I told him."

Poor Chicken. He'd never been away from Mom so long; neither of them had.

"But you promised you would teach me to fish." Cat's voice cracked; she was trying not to cry.

"I'm sorry," said Mom. "Work comes first."

Cat was quiet. She knew that work came first. But sometimes it felt like Cat came last.

"Listen," Mom was saying. "You'll have to take care of your hair."

And that was another thing. Cat closed her eyes. "Mom, I don't know where to start."

"You have your conditioner and comb, right? Take your time and work out every tangle. I mean every single one."

"But what about my braid? I can't do it myself," said Cat. She'd tried before, but she couldn't reach. Plus, her arms got too tired.

Mom sighed. "Do two ponytails instead of a French braid. Maybe braid each one. You can do that, right?"

Maybe. But Mom knew Cat liked a French braid best. "I guess."

"You'll have to make it work, Cat. Find a video online and ask your grandma to help."

No way. When Cat was small, Daddy had combed and braided her hair. After he died, Mom took over. It had taken months for her to learn to do it right. Lily couldn't learn in a day, even if it was something Cat wanted—which she did not.

"I'll handle it," Cat said finally.

"I better run," said Mom. "Everyone's waiting for me. Love you."

Cat disconnected. Now that Mom wasn't on the line anymore, the tears wanted to come. She sniffed.

"You shouldn't give her a hard time," Macon said. "She has a work commitment—a big honor. You should be proud of her."

Cat flinched, like the words had bitten her. "I *am* proud."

Lily gave Macon a pointed look and then turned to Cat. "It's okay to be disappointed. Doesn't mean you aren't proud."

Macon took his mug to the sink. "Maybe she can give you fishing tips over the phone."

He didn't understand. She needed Mom. Fishing tips over the phone wouldn't give that special side-by-side time.

Lily seemed to read Cat's expression. "I'm sure the two of you will figure it out."

"I'm heading to bed," Cat said. She said good night and clomped upstairs. First, she checked on Chicken in the guest room, who lay on his back with his arms and legs spread out straight. No wonder he kicked her so often, if he wanted to sleep that stretched out. She decided to sleep in the very center of the bed since she didn't have to share that night. Her eyes traced every bump and crack of the ceiling.

Her thoughts turned over on themselves until they were a tangled mess. Mom couldn't teach Cat to fish long distance. If Cat backed out of the contest, John Harvey would laugh at her for quitting. But if she showed up and didn't catch a single fish, John Harvey would laugh at her for that. She was tired of coming in last. She couldn't let that happen.

When she heard her door open, Cat's brain was buzzing, but she pretended to be asleep. At first, she thought it was Chicken, but the footsteps were too careful. It was Lily. She tucked Cat in, kissed her on the forehead, and was gone again in a flash.

PART THREE
Gather & Hunt

Together is my very favorite place to be.

—Caterpillar in *Caterpillar & Chicken: Friends for Infinity*

13

Sandpipers dashed in and out of the waves, gobbling unlucky fish. Cat wasn't sure she'd be welcome on the morning walk, but Macon had been waiting for her like normal.

"I didn't like the way we left things last night," said Macon.

She leaned over to pick up a plastic cup.

"And now you're awful quiet," he said.

Cat shrugged. It was easier to be quiet.

Finally, Macon cleared his throat. "Are you . . . ah . . . disappointed about your mom?"

"I'm not supposed to be, right? Just proud," said Cat.

Macon scratched the back of his neck. "You should be proud. It's not easy to support a family. She works hard."

Cat dug her toes in the sand. He didn't get it. "I'm tired of work coming first."

"I'll take the blame for that one," Macon said.

Cat glanced at him. He squinted at the water like he saw something far away. "Surgeons don't have dependable schedules. Lots of times I broke promises. I guess that's why it was hard to see you disappointed."

That must have been what Mom meant when she said Macon was never around.

"Did you fix it?" she asked. "Did you change your schedule?"

Macon pushed his ball cap lower. "Mostly I stopped making promises."

Cat frowned. "I thought you said half of life is showing up. What does it mean if you weren't around?"

When she saw his face, she felt like she'd gone too far. He looked like a half-empty balloon.

"If I could go back, I'd do it differently," he said.

They turned and walked to the house.

It was fifteen steps before Cat reached for his hand.

It was rough and scratchy. It fit okay.

14

Lily called it pimento cheese, but Cat was suspicious.

She prodded the orange mound. "Doesn't look like any cheese I've ever seen."

Chicken patted it with his spoon. "It's a glob," he announced. "It's glob-cheese."

Lily shook her head, but she was smiling. "Some things look good and some things taste good. I'd pick taste every time."

"More for me," said Macon, smiling, and reached toward Chicken's plate as if he was going to take it.

This worked. Chicken shoveled it in. His eyes widened, and he scooped again.

"It's better than it looks," he said around a mouthful.

Cat tried it. Smooth, with a sharp kick at the end. She had another bite. Lily's kitchen was a delicious place to be.

They were still eating when there was a knock at the door—Harriet. In one hand she held three fishing nets and in the other, a bucket with a jumble of mini flashlights.

Cat raised her eyebrows. There was no way those nets would work from the pier.

"You sounded sorta blue about your mom, so I came up with a plan." Harriet looked past Cat. "You all having supper?"

"Good evening, Harriet," said Lily. "Join us, won't you?"

"Hey, Ms. Lily," said Harriet. "I already ate, thanks." But she pulled out a chair, eyeing the food.

"Nonsense," said Lily, placing a plate in front of her.

"Well, maybe I've got room." Harriet dug in.

Lily grinned. "Tell me about all this stuff."

Harriet wiped her mouth. "Yesterday was a bad day fishing, and today Cat's having a bad day, period. We need something to change our luck," said Harriet.

Lily looked puzzled. "Night fishing?"

"Not fishing," said Harriet, grinning. "*Hunting.*"

A grin spread over Macon's tanned face, transforming it into a map of creases and wrinkles.

"Think it's warm enough?" he asked Harriet.

"I reckon so, it's practically July."

"What are y'all talking about?" said Lily.

At the same time, Harriet and Macon said, "Ghost crabbing!"

"Ghost crabbing?" asked Cat. "What's that?"

"You don't know ghost crabs?" asked Harriet between bites. "They mostly hide during the day, but sometimes they pop out for a spell. They're the same color as the sand—with little eyeballs that stick up." Harriet scuttled her hand across the table.

"But why are they called ghost crabs?" asked Chicken.

"It's 'cause they come out at night!" Harriet stretched out the last word to make it sound spooky. "Or maybe because they're pale. Who knows." Chicken laughed.

Harriet continued. "When a flashlight shines on the sand, you see hundreds of eyes looking back at you."

"Creepy," said Cat.

"But not scary," said Harriet.

"Can I come along?" asked Chicken.

"But you don't like lots of eyes looking at you," said Cat, remembering his comment about Toy Boat's action figures.

"I don't mind *crab* eyes," Chicken said. There was no understanding him sometimes.

"I'm in," said Macon, surprising Cat. "Lily, what do you say?"

"Only if Chicken promises to hold my hand," said Lily. "If we lose you in the dark we'll never find you."

"I promise," said Chicken solemnly.

Harriet distributed the flashlights. The sand was cool and damp under Cat's feet. At first there was nothing. But then, in a beam of light—

"There's one!" called Harriet. She scurried after a crab

the size of a quarter, which disappeared into its burrow before Harriet could reach it.

"There, Caterpillar, there!" called Chicken, pointing his flashlight.

The beam illuminated a group scurrying sideways across the sandy terrain. She raced after them. The one closest to her was the largest. She smacked her net down. "I got one!" she shouted.

Harriet was there in a flash. "Let's see."

"Turn it slowly over the bucket," said Macon.

Harriet held the bucket steady. With a plop, the crab landed inside.

Chicken aimed his flashlight. "Get me another, Caterpillar, please!"

Cat and Harriet dashed along the shore, chasing the funny little ghost crabs. They brought their prisoners to Chicken, who proudly guarded the bucket. Finally, they counted them.

"Twenty-three!" said Chicken, in awe.

"Time to call it a night," said Lily. Chicken handed the bucket to the girls and went back to the house with Lily. Cat found herself wishing he'd fall asleep in the guest room bed again.

"Ready to let go?" Harriet asked.

"Later, ghost crabs," said Cat. They tipped the bucket slowly. Crabs scuttled in all directions.

"May you never eat a baby sea turtle," added Harriet.

"The unlucky streak is officially broken," said Cat. "Next up, catching an actual fish!"

They walked Harriet to the corner. She crashed the screen door open and disappeared into the house. There was no way to miss Harriet coming or going.

"What do you think?" asked Macon. "Will that do the trick?"

Cat didn't know, but she could hope. She would find out tomorrow.

15

Chicken was a creative sleeper. He had fallen asleep in the guest room, just as she'd hoped, and in the morning she checked on him. This time he had turned sideways so his feet hung off the side of the bed. He made a whistling sound when he breathed out. Two nights of Chicken in his own bed was a major victory. Maybe it was all the delicious food. Maybe it was the ocean air.

When Cat came downstairs, Lily looked at her, eyebrows arched.

"Did he go on a walk without you?"

"I told him to go ahead," said Cat. She picked up the mug of hot chocolate he'd left for her. "I'm meeting Harriet early because it's supposed to rain later."

"Let me make you a sandwich," said Lily. She built a biscuit stuffed with ham and eggs.

Cat gave her a quick hug. "Thanks."

When she opened the door, Macon was coming upstairs.

"Howdy," said Macon.

"Hey," said Cat. She was already down the steps and three houses down the path when he called after her.

"Good luck!" he shouted.

"Thank you!" Cat called back. She saw Harriet and broke into a careful run. When she caught up, she handed Harriet half her sandwich. At the pier, John Harvey had claimed his lucky spot at the end. Just to annoy them, he announced every catch he made, each one seemingly bigger than the last.

"Silent treatment," Harriet whispered. "Let's freeze him out."

But John Harvey didn't care. Each time he announced another fish, Harriet got angrier. Finally, she was boiling. "I wish I knew what we were doing wrong!" She pointed at a small building adjacent to the pier. "I know we don't have money, but let's check out the bait shop. Dean should give us some advice. Or, even if he can't, we'll have a break from hearing John Harvey, and that's worth something."

They pushed open the shop door. A grizzled man sat behind the counter. "Morning, ladies," he said, looking up from his copy of the *Weekly Wave*.

"Hey, Dean," said Harriet. "This is my friend Cat."

Dean folded the newspaper. "Hey there, Cat. Are you Amanda's girl?"

Cat nodded, wondering how he knew.

"Miss her something fierce around here," said Dean. "It's a shame we haven't seen her in so long. She was a right good fisherman, and a good girl, too." He shook his head.

"We need advice," said Harriet, plunking down at the counter. "We can't catch a fish for the life of us."

Dean rubbed his chin, seeming to understand this was a serious situation. "What y'all been using as bait?"

"Hot dogs mostly," said Cat. "Also cornbread."

Dean rubbed his chin, thinking. "Crumbly?"

The girls nodded.

"Let me see what I have in the back." He dug in a freezer case, finally returning with a bag of silvery fish.

"Take these anchovies. Free sample to get you started." Dean put them in another bag and knotted the top. "Should work better than hot dogs and cornbread."

"That's so nice," said Cat as she took the bag. "Thank you."

She wanted to ask more questions, about fishing or maybe about her mom, but when the door jangled, Dean went to talk with his customers.

Back on the pier, John Harvey and Dixie had gone. Good.

"All right." Cat tried to sound confident. Her experience with anchovies was seeing them on Mom's half of the pizza, where they lay there, smelly and shriveled.

These anchovies were torpedo-shaped and larger than she expected. They also had faces and tails.

"Ugh," said Harriet. "Their dead eyes."

Cat grimaced. She found a hook, then knotted it to the fishing line. She took a fish from the package and pushed the hook tentatively, but it didn't go in. Harriet shrugged.

Again, Cat pushed and this time it sunk into the fish. She shuddered, dropping her line in so she didn't have to look at it.

Harriet whistled. "Wow, Cat, you look like a real fisherman. A real fisherperson, I mean."

Cat grinned. Today her luck might turn around. There was something about using real bait that felt official. Mom would be impressed if Cat figured out fishing on her own. Cat wouldn't tell her beforehand, she would just bait her hook like it was no big thing.

Harriet crossed her arms and turned up the side of her mouth. "Hey, girls," she drawled, sounding so much like John Harvey that Cat expected to see Harriet's freckles disappear and her eyelashes turn blond. "Just wanted y'all to know that I caught a million fish today. Naw, make it a billion."

"A trillion," said Cat in her best Southern accent.

"A squillion." Harriet stretched out her hands.

"A googolplex!"

"A googolplex . . . plus one!" said Harriet.

This was too much. Cat cracked up.

"John Harvey is the worst," she said. "The only good thing about him is his dog."

They leaned against the railing, laughing.

Behind them was a jingling sound. Cat hoped it was the door from Dean's bait shop, or maybe the tags of some other dog. But when she glanced back, Dixie was trotting along behind John Harvey, who was returning to his lucky spot at the end of the pier.

Cat's cheeks were hot. "Do you think he heard us?"

Harriet shrugged. "He says worse stuff than that each morning before breakfast."

Cat and Harriet had been having fun. And he had been so nasty anyway, did it really matter if his feelings were hurt? She tried to push away that did-something-bad feeling, but it stuck like bubble gum. It had taken some of the fun out of the morning.

Cat checked her line, but when she reeled it in, her bait was gone. She brought it all the way in and rehooked a different fish, closer to the tail this time. But again, it disappeared from the hook without Cat feeling it. As the day got warmer, the bait got mushy and was harder to hook. She tried until the anchovies were gone, but they didn't catch a single fish. They didn't even get a nibble.

John Harvey, of course, caught a ton. He stopped announcing each one, but it was obvious how busy he was.

"I wish I knew what we were doing wrong," said Cat.

"Yeah," said Harriet. "Me too. We need our own lucky spot."

A lucky spot. Lucky bait. Cat didn't consider herself lucky. She wanted to surprise Mom with how much she had learned, but at this rate it would never happen. As much fun as Harriet was, Cat needed someone to show her what to do. Mom couldn't help if she was never here. Somehow, Cat would have to figure it out on her own.

16

Thunder rumbled over the ocean and rain came in thick drops. Lily tapped at her laptop while Macon read the *Weekly Wave*. Chicken sat in the laundry basket, reading a book about shark researcher Eugenie Clark. Cat sighed.

Macon folded the newspaper. "Anyone want to go get an ice cream?"

"I'll go," said Cat.

Chicken didn't look up. "No thanks, I'm at the good part. And I've got these." He patted a stack of slick-jacketed library books.

Lily closed her laptop with a click. "I think Chicken's got the right idea—it's the perfect day for reading."

Chicken pointed to the other end of the basket. "Come in my boat."

Lily sat next to him on the floor with her paperback. "I think I'll float in the ocean next to you instead, Captain." Chicken giggled.

Cat was learning to trust Lily. She was good with Chicken, and paid attention to what he needed. Still, Cat double-checked that the sliding door was locked before she left. She didn't want Chicken to get any ideas about conducting some shark research while she was gone.

Together she and Macon went down the white wooden staircase. He handed her an umbrella. It wasn't very big. Before she could offer to share, Macon cinched the draw-strings on his hood. "That's all right. I'll walk behind so I don't crowd you."

"I don't mind—"

But he gestured for her to go ahead. She felt silly walking that way, like they were a tiny parade of two people. Macon only made sense on their beach walks. Other than that he remained a mystery.

Rainwater flowed down the road. As they passed Willis General, Macon tapped her shoulder. "Your grandmother said we need hot sauce. I'll duck in here."

Cat turned to follow, but he stopped her.

"Go on ahead," he said. "Have some samples and I'll be right there."

Before Cat could answer, he disappeared into the store. Sometimes he seemed like he wanted to spend time with her. Other times, he would disappear just like that.

She continued to the ice cream shop by herself. The letters spelling out "Miss Sunshine's" looked like they were made of pink and yellow sprinkles. Cat shook the umbrella the best she could before pushing open the door.

A woman in a pink apron looked up, a smile ready. The place was empty, maybe because of the rain. When she saw Cat, her smile froze for a half second but then looked normal again. "Welcome to Miss Sunshine's," she called in a sugary sweet voice.

"Hi." Cat looked around.

Everything was yellow or pink—the checkered floor, the pinstriped walls, the booths and counter stools. Even the topping jars had yellow and pink labels.

The woman, who was older than Mom but younger than Macon and Lily, squirted a cleaner on the counter and wiped it with a yellow cloth. Even the spray cleaner was pink. Miss Sunshine's hair was yellow and her fingernails were pink. It was the most carefully color-coordinated place Cat had seen, and it made her kind of uncomfortable.

She walked to the case to see the flavors. Ever since she was small, her favorite had been mint chocolate chip, but she thought she might try their special flavors, which included Gingerbread Island and Turtle Egg. She examined each container and reread the labels three times, but still the woman didn't come over to ask her what she'd like.

The door jangled open. Macon smiled, holding up a Willis General bag.

The woman at the counter put down the squirt bottle. "Why, *hello* Dr. Stone," she said. The *hello* was all stretched out and sounded like "hey-low." If her voice was sugary before, this sounded downright sticky. "Can't *believe* we are so empty the one day you come in. I promise we usually have more customers."

Cat tried not to stare. Miss Sunshine looked at Macon like he was a movie star. *Gross.*

Macon didn't seem to notice. "Ah, yes. Well. My grand-children are in town."

"You should bring them in," trilled the lady.

Macon's forehead wrinkled in confusion. "I did," he said slowly. "This is my granddaughter, Cat."

"Oh," said the ice cream lady, looking back and forth. "Oh! I didn't know you all knew each other."

Sometimes that happened with Mom, where people didn't know that she was connected to Cat and Chicken. But this was the first time it happened with Macon. Cat waited to see what he would say, but he didn't react. He stood next to her and peered through the glass. "Which samples have you tried so far?"

"None," Cat answered.

"*None?*" Macon glanced at Cat, then at the cup filled with taster spoons. He looked at Miss Sunshine and then at Cat again. His forehead wrinkles went deeper for an instant and then cleared, like he understood something.

He put his hand on Cat's shoulder, and aimed a smile at

Miss Sunshine. It wasn't his usual crinkle-eyed smile. This was a smile Cat had never seen. It was more of a toothpaste commercial smile. "Miss Campbell, isn't it?"

"Call me Parker," the woman singsonged.

Cat looked at her curiously. She couldn't tell if Parker was her first name or her last name. It didn't matter though, because Cat would probably always think of her as Miss Sunshine.

"Miss Parker," he said. His tone was smooth, and suddenly his Southern accent became stronger. That was interesting, because Mom always got extremely polite and very Southern when she was hopping mad on the inside. Cat looked at him out of the corner of her eye.

He still had the toothpaste smile. "Could my granddaughter, Cat, and I get some samples? She needs a big Gingerbread Island welcome, so I think it would be best for her to have a sample of *every* flavor."

Cat's eyes widened. There had to be at least thirty tubs of ice cream. Cat tried to keep her expression casual, like it was normal to have thirty samples of ice cream—no big deal.

Miss Sunshine's smile faltered for a second but then sugared up full strength. "Of course! She's *precious*, Dr. Stone. Let me get some samples for y'all."

Spoon after spoon the samples came, and they were all for Cat. Miss Sunshine tried to hand some to Macon, but he waved them away, saying he knew what he wanted. The

158

entire time Cat sampled, his hand stayed steady on her shoulder, like he was reminding Cat that he was there.

The ice cream was rich and creamy. Turtle Egg was chocolate-caramel eggs with a raspberry ribbon. The Gingerbread Island flavor had gum drops and tiny gingerbread people. She tried each flavor, even though cotton candy bubble gum twist hurt her teeth.

Cat's tongue couldn't keep track of all the flavors, so she settled on her old favorite, mint chocolate chip. She was glad her ice cream wasn't yellow or pink. Macon got lemon-blueberry. Miss Sunshine scooped with a smile, and agreed to hold Chicken's rainbow sherbet in the freezer until they were ready to walk home.

Cat and Macon picked a pink booth in the window. Sheets of water poured from the awning. Of course no one was at the playground, and the library didn't seem to have any business either. It was like the downtown belonged to the two of them, and of course Miss Sunshine, who had gone back to scrubbing her counter.

Immediately Cat peeled the wrapper from the cone, because it was always the first thing she did. She should have been full from all the samples, but she'd saved some room.

If Mom were here, they would talk about the way Miss Sunshine became a hundred times friendlier after Macon walked in. It could have been prejudice against what Cat looked like. It could have been ageism, since she was young and by herself. Or maybe it could have been something else entirely—but Cat didn't think so. It was hard to untangle the threads of why someone acted the way they did.

She didn't know how to talk about it with Macon, or even if she should. She couldn't tell what he thought, what the toothpaste smile had meant exactly. But her shoulder was still warm where his hand had been, and that counted for something.

Macon chomped his ice cream, finishing before Cat. He tore the wrapper in tiny shreds.

Cat nibbled her cone. "Think it will stop pretty soon?"

He looked startled, like she had interrupted his thoughts. "Sorry, what did you say?"

Cat pointed out the window. "The rain. Think it will blow over soon?"

"Probably," he said absentmindedly. "Anyway. I've been thinking." He cleared his throat. "It's been such a long time for me. With fishing, I mean."

Cat's insides tightened. His timing was terrible. Even though it had started awkwardly, they'd had a good time getting ice cream. She would always remember trying all those samples. But here he was, bringing up fishing, just to tell her no *again*.

Macon took a deep breath. "Half of life is showing up, and it's the same with fishing. You have been doing a great job with that."

Cat laughed shortly. If he was giving her credit for showing up, he might as well give her a prize for breathing. Sure, she'd shown up, but hadn't caught a single fish. It didn't seem like anything to be excited about.

"Big deal," she said.

"Hey," he said seriously. "Not every kid would keep trying. You've got grit—gumption." He drummed his fingers on the tabletop. "In fact, I decided it's not fair that you're trying so hard and I'm not trying at all. So I was thinking I could try, too."

Cat looked at him carefully. "Really?"

"No promises," he said. "But I'll teach you what I can."

They were quiet. The rain poured. Back on the beach, he told her he'd stopped making promises. But she remembered his voice when he'd said "my granddaughter, Cat." It hadn't sounded like someone who was afraid of promises.

They could do this. And, although maybe it was too much to hope for, Mom might join them when she visited. Then it would be three of them, side by side.

"One question," she said.

Macon swept the wrapper pieces into his hand. "Anything."

"When do we start?"

17

Even in the soft morning light, Macon was still the most rectangular person she had ever met. Blocky and solid, he stood on the deck, waiting for her. Cat moved quickly and silently down the stairs. It would be their first morning fishing.

When Macon saw her, he smiled. "Good. The early bird gets the worm, the early worm gets the fish, and all that."

In the driveway, Macon divided the gear between their bikes and together they rode to the bait shop. Macon held the door for Cat.

"Howdy, Macon," said Dean. It was the same man who had given Cat and Harriet the anchovies.

"This is my granddaughter, Cat," said Macon. "She's with us for a bit this summer."

Dean nodded. "She takes after her mama, doesn't she?

That's a good thing, Cat—you don't want to look like this old bird."

Macon laughed. "She and I are more alike than you know. Did you know this one's been teaching herself to fish? Along with the help of little Miss Harriet Kincaid."

Dean winked. "I may have seen the two of them around the pier. Are you going to give that John Harvey a run for his money?"

"I hope to," said Cat.

"That's the spirit," said Dean. "Glad you're teaching her, Macon. That's one of the benefits of being a grandfather. What can I help y'all with today?"

Dean and Macon had a long discussion about shrimp, anchovies, and finger mullet. Cat drifted over to the rack of sunglasses.

Macon opened the door. "Ready, Cat?" They walked onto the pier.

Macon paused. "Do you have a favorite place?"

"We move around. We haven't found a lucky spot yet," said Cat.

"Sometimes you can make your own luck." He pointed to a cluster of birds flying over the water. "Why do you think they're all hanging around?"

That was easy—the birds on the beach were interested in one thing.

"Food," said Cat.

"Attagirl," said Macon.

They moved closer to the gulls. Macon unwrapped the

package from the bait store and emptied it into a bucket. When Cat looked she was surprised to see shrimp—live ones.

Macon added a frozen water bottle to the bucket. "They like cooler temperatures," he explained. "Depending on how long we're here, we may need to change their water. Don't let me forget."

He was careful with the little creatures, and Cat liked that. She tied the fishing line to her hook, and he pointed out a few adjustments to her knots. Before the contest, Cat thought fishing sounded easy. Talking with Macon made her realize there was so much to learn.

Macon picked up a squirming shrimp. "I'll hook the first one for you." He pointed at a dark area on the shrimp's head. "Never go through here, this is the brain. Push the hook through this spiky part on the top, which is called the horn."

Macon slowly moved the hook through to the shrimp's tail. For as big as his fingers were, they were surprisingly light and careful. Cat easily imagined the same hands doing surgery, sewing people up, helping them.

"Why do you hook it there?" she asked.

"Shrimp kick backward when they are fleeing from a predator, so this gives it a more natural look. Plus, in my experience, it stays on better. The fish we're trying for is called a sheepshead—one of the trickiest, bait-stealing fish in these waters."

Cat's eyes widened. She couldn't catch a regular fish,

and now he wanted her to catch a clever one? It seemed impossible.

He laughed at her expression. "Don't worry—you've got a fighting chance. The fish love to hang out near the pier. The pilings create little nooks and crannies the fish love. Let your line go straight down, even underneath the pier if you can."

Cat liked how he explained things. He didn't treat her like a little kid, but he didn't act like she was already supposed to know what to do.

Macon fastened a pyramid-shaped sinker on the line. "If you ever see a patch of cloudy water, aim right for it. The fish will fight each other to get the bait."

They spent some time in peaceful silence. This was that side-by-side time Cat wanted so much. They felt like a team working together. She hoped they would catch a fish. It didn't have to be a tricky one. Anything would do.

Her line tugged and whirred. Cat froze, looking at Macon.

"Get one?" he asked.

"I think so?"

His voice was calm. "Slow and steady."

Cat turned the crank. She couldn't believe how strong the fish was.

"He's putting up a big fight," Macon said. "You can do it, Cat."

The fish rose out of the water, wiggling and twisting. The scales glinted in the morning sun as she reeled it in. Finally, it reached the edge of the railing and she pulled it onto the pier. "I did it!"

Macon removed the hook. The fish had bold vertical stripes all along its sides.

"Good job," he said to Cat. "Got him in without breaking the line; that's not easy. This is a sheepshead, also called a convict fish—see the stripes?"

"Now what?" Cat asked.

"We can release it or we can eat it," said Macon. "And I think a fisherman has a duty to eat her first fish. Besides, this fellow is good eating."

Cat nodded. "Macon? Can we fish a little more before we head back?"

The corners of Macon's mouth twitched up. "Of course. Whatever you like."

They fished for a while longer and caught a bluefish, but they let it go. The sheepshead would be their lunch. Not bad for a few hours of fishing.

"Go on home," Macon told her. "I'll clean it—they're a pain to clean—I'll be after you in a bit."

Cat pedaled to the house, cool air whipping her face until it stung. Her heart soared. She replayed the moment she felt the pull on the line. Landing it was a struggle, but she'd done it. Things were turning around with fishing. Things were turning around with the whole summer.

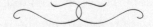

Cat exploded inside the kitchen door. "I got two fish!"

"Yay, Cat!" said Chicken.

Lily got up from the sofa. "Wonderful, Cat. What kind?"

"A bluefish and a sheepshead," she said. She looked at Chicken. "You'd like the sheepshead, Chicken. It's striped."

Cat turned back to Lily. "We released the bluefish, but Macon is cleaning the sheepshead down at the pier."

"We'll have it for lunch, then." Lily peered inside the pantry. "I'm out of cornmeal—are you up for a trip to Willis General?"

"Sure," said Cat. "Chicken, do you want to go with me?"

Chicken thought for a moment.

"Or you can stay and help me make lunch," offered Lily.

Chicken nodded. "I want to stay."

Cat kept her surprise to herself and took the stairs two at a time to the driveway. Chicken liked cooking with Lily. She was glad for them to have their special thing, like she had with Macon.

Cat decided to take her bike. She was so excited, she could practically fly. Finally! And not just one fish, but two!

Cat went downstairs for her bike, then rode downtown. Her hands still felt the sensation of the fish pulling on the line. Maybe she'd bump into Harriet and could tell her the news right away. She leaned her bike in the alley around the corner from Willis General, and pushed open the glossy green door.

"Hey there, Cat," said Ms. Willis.

"Hi, Ms. Willis."

"Let me know if you need anything."

Cat took the long way to the food aisles. She smelled several bars of soap, sidestepped a display overflowing with bouncing balls, and examined some dangling spider plants before she found the shelf with cornmeal. She carried it up to the counter.

Ms. Willis gave Cat the total. "Your grandma making cornbread?"

"It's for my fish," said Cat. "I caught two this morning."

"Hooray!" Ms. Willis sounded genuinely happy for her. "Are you excited for the contest?"

Cat nodded. "My grandpa said he's going to teach me every day."

"I love that," said Ms. Willis. "Say hi to your grandma for me."

As Cat walked back to the alleyway, she realized she had called Macon her grandpa. The word came out easily, like he had been hers for a long time. The thought made her happy. But then she saw her bike.

At first, she didn't recognize it. The paint was no longer lemon yellow. It was brown. A layer of mud covered every inch of the frame and seat. The flowered basket hung crookedly. Circling around the bike, Cat stopped suddenly. The Amanda license plate was missing. She checked the ground, to see if it had fallen or been thrown to the side, but it wasn't there. Someone had stolen it.

Cat stalked to the main street and saw a tourist family and a woman with a jogging stroller. She walked another block, turned a corner, and came face-to-face with Harriet.

Harriet's big grin faded quickly. "What's wrong?"

"Come see," said Cat, through clenched teeth. They walked back to the bike.

Harriet gasped. "Aww, no, your beautiful bike! And your basket's all cattywampus."

Cat tried to straighten it, but it was stuck at an odd angle. She felt like throwing the cornmeal sack against the wall.

Suddenly, Harriet let out a low whistle. "Are you thinking what I'm thinking?"

Cat said, "Do you mean *who* you're thinking?"

"Cat, look!" From the puddle in the alleyway a row of paw prints led to the street. Paw prints of a familiar size.

"Dixie," breathed Cat.

"Where are you hiding, John Harvey?" bellowed Harriet. "I'm about to cloud up and rain on you."

Cat frowned. "Wait."

Harriet clenched her fists. "I'm not afraid to fight him."

"I don't want to fight him. At least not in that way."

Harriet's eyes shined. "How then?"

"The contest," said Cat.

Harriet looked doubtful. "No offense, Cat, but you haven't caught anything yet."

"That changed today," said Cat. "Macon took me and I caught two."

"If you win, it'll hurt him where it counts," said Harriet.

For the first time, Cat could see herself winning. She couldn't wait to see the look on John Harvey's face when she walked away with the trophy.

She said good-bye to Harriet and wheeled her bike home. After giving Lily the cornmeal, Cat went downstairs and found rags, soap, and a bucket. She was lugging the heavy bucket when Macon came down the white wooden staircase.

"Your grandmother's cooking the fish."

Cat started scrubbing. "Good."

Macon regarded her for a minute and then picked up a rag. He dunked it in the soapy water and wiped the handlebars. "Bike need a wash?"

"Yep."

"That's a lot of mud on there."

"Yep." Cat scrubbed at a stubborn bit of dirt.

"Musta been some puddle," he said.

Cat looked at the ground. She didn't want him to think she hadn't taken care of the beautiful yellow bike. "It looked like this when I came out of Willis General."

"That's a shame," said Macon.

Cat nodded and didn't say anything else. She wasn't a tattler.

Little by little they wiped away at the mud and the bike returned to its former, gleaming state. Lily called down the stairs that lunch was ready.

Macon didn't mention the missing license plate. Neither did Cat.

18

The next morning, Cat and Macon fished for hours, and released them all. She was barely in the door when Chicken ran into her, almost knocking her down. "Chicken! What's going on?"

He hoisted a large envelope in the air. "Mama's practice book came!"

"Oh, it did? How exciting. Did you look at it already?"

He shook his head.

"He insisted on waiting for you," said Lily.

"We always look at them together," said Cat. "But I'm sandy from digging on the beach. Can you wait for me to get washed off? I will be right back down."

He narrowed his eyes. "How many minutes?"

"Eight?"

His eyes got narrower.

"Okay, five . . . three?"

He nodded and eyed the kitchen clock. Cat raced upstairs, knowing he would hold her to the time limit. She was actually excited to see this one. Mom hadn't shown her much of it, but she remembered that it was something about hats.

When she came back downstairs, Chicken was sitting crisscross by the living room window. She sat next to him on the floor and pulled the review copy of Mom's new book out of the envelope.

Chicken and Caterpillar were on the front cover.

"The Best Hat," read Chicken.

"Do you want to read it or should I?" asked Cat.

"You do it," he said, squishing up next to her.

The story began with Cat and Chicken on a bus, heading to a hat store where a big sale was taking place. After the first page, she stopped in surprise. When she read the title, she assumed it would be Chicken who would get the best hat, but she was wrong. It was *Caterpillar* who had saved her money and couldn't wait to pick out the perfect hat. She looked adorable holding her tiny pocketbook. Finally, Caterpillar was going to do something for herself, instead of saving the day for someone else.

Caterpillar tried on a bunch of different hats. Finally, she decided on a funny one with long chin straps. The drawing of Caterpillar, beaming in her new hat, made Cat grin. The hat looked like one Cat had in fourth grade.

But then Chicken showed up at the hat shop. He looked at Caterpillar, who was wearing her new hat.

"It's a nice hat," he said. "But . . ."

Cat frowned. But?

. . . my beak is cold.

"Caterpillar, this book is so funny!" he gasped.

"Yeah . . . funny." Cat pushed it aside. Chicken picked it up.

"Can we read it again?"

"Hmmm, why don't you read it to me this time?"

He took the pages and started reading out loud. Cat lowered herself to the floor and lay down next to Chicken. He put his fingers in her hair. She closed her eyes as she listened to him read. Suddenly, he shook her shoulder.

"Are you awake?"

"Yeah. Just thinking."

"You can't see the pictures if your eyes are closed," he pointed out.

She opened her eyes. "I remember what they look like."

"Well, don't you like Mama's book?" Chicken sounded impatient.

"I feel bad for Caterpillar."

Chicken held up the book. "There aren't any cookies. No symbols."

Cat rubbed her eyes and stretched. She was tired. Maybe she'd had too much sun. "Don't worry, Chicken. I think it's a great book."

"I'm not worried," said Chicken. "When Chicken is happy, Caterpillar is happy. Chicken's job is being happy and Caterpillar's job is making him happy."

This was exactly what Cat was afraid of. She hoped Mom didn't see her as someone who existed just to make

Chicken happy. She had her own thoughts, her own ideas, her own things she liked that had nothing to do with Chicken.

"You know it's a book, right?" Cat asked. "It's a made-up story."

Chicken ignored her. "Lily, did you hear Mama's book?"

"I did," said Lily, looking up from her papers.

"I want to show it to Macon." He went upstairs.

It's a book. Just a book. Cat kept telling herself that, hoping it would start to seem like the truth.

PART FOUR
Answers & Questions

Of all the chickens in the world, I'm so glad I have you.

—Caterpillar in *Caterpillar & Chicken: The Marmalade Mystery*

19

Cat wasn't sure if fish were shy or stubborn, but some mornings she and Macon came away empty-handed, even after spending hours at the pier. They had been there since the sun came up and the fish weren't cooperating. She focused on the water, hoping a hungry fish would find her hook.

The time spent with Macon was often her favorite part of the day. The stillness of the morning surrounded them, and the sound of rushing waves made her breathe deeper. She leaned back on the bench and let her mind wander to the day she'd arrived on the island. She had so many questions about why Mom left, and here she was ten days later without any answers.

"How come you and Mom never talk?" The words were out before she realized them.

Macon rubbed the rough, tanned skin at the back of his neck. "She talks to your grandma."

It was too late to go back; she had to go forward. "But she never talks to you."

"That's a tough one." He was quiet for a long time, looking at the water. Cat was starting to think he had forgotten the question.

Finally, he spoke. "Promise to stay and hear me out?"

"Of course."

Macon shifted on the bench, pulling his old blue ball cap down over his eyes. "When your mom and dad got married—I didn't take the news well."

A picture from the Big Blue Book floated into her brain—the wedding day on the courthouse steps. "Why?"

"I wanted more for her."

Cat frowned. "How?"

"I thought of art as a hobby, not a career," he said. "I wanted her to have stability, thought she should consider pre-med."

Mom as a doctor? She could never pick the right medicine for someone or do surgery. She didn't even like to be around sick people. Mom made things that were funny and beautiful, and constantly had paint under her fingernails.

Cat shook her head. "Never in a million years."

Macon chuckled. "So that part wasn't the greatest idea. But there was more. They came to see us. I'd never seen Amanda so excited. Ben wore a tie." He stopped for a minute.

"I thought he was going to ask for her hand in marriage," Macon continued, finally. "I would have asked them to wait a bit longer. They were so young. But . . ."

Cat frowned. "But what?"

He grimaced. "They weren't asking. They'd eloped, ran off and gotten married without telling their families. And that wasn't even their biggest news."

Cat knew immediately. "Me. I was their biggest news, right? They were expecting me."

Macon nodded. He didn't meet her eye.

She understood in a flash. Macon said he didn't agree with Mom's choices. That meant being an artist, marrying Daddy—and one more thing. Mom's choice to have Cat. Sharp tears prickled her eyes. No wonder he shut himself away when they arrived. He had never wanted her to be born.

She stood. Even though her knees wobbled, she would go. She did not want him to see her cry.

Macon's voice was quiet. "Hear me out."

She hesitated.

"Please," he repeated, voice scratchy.

It was the "please" that did it. She lowered herself to the bench.

"Thank you," he said sadly. "The first thing you need to know is that your grandpa is a stubborn old fool."

Her mouth almost twitched into a smile, but the dull ache in her heart smoothed it into a line.

Macon continued, "My plan for your mom's life did not

include a husband and a child, living on the other side of the dadgum country. In San Francisco!"

She crossed her arms. There was nothing wrong with Mom, Daddy, or San Francisco. There was nothing wrong with Cat.

"I was coming at it all wrong. I saw Amanda as a child, my child. Not as a person who was on her own path—on a path with your dad."

Macon sighed. "I followed the steps. Your mom was supposed to follow them, too. College before marriage. Marriage before babies. That's how I thought it should be done."

Cat shook her head. "Because it was right for you doesn't mean it was right for her. For them."

Macon took off his hat and waved it. "Where the heck were you when I needed to hear that twelve years ago?"

She looked at his face. Through his tears, his eyes twinkled. Cat couldn't help it. She grinned back at him. She thought of the girl Mom had been on this island: her white dress and gloves, her school pictures on the wall. It didn't seem like Macon had known that girl very well.

"So what happened?" Cat said. "Exactly, I mean."

Macon let out a long breath. "They wanted to run off into the sunset together. No plans, no jobs, no apartment. The only thing they were sure of was each other."

Her beautiful young parents, so in love, so ready to be a family.

Macon sighed again. "I reacted badly. That's an understatement. My feelings were hurt, I see that. I tried to lay down the law—like she was a child—because I was afraid to lose her. And in doing that, I really did lose her."

They looked at the water. For the first time ever, Cat was glad the fish weren't biting.

"After she left, I was angry," said Macon. "That's when I started my morning walks. The ocean heard my anger, and eventually washed it away. Then I finally understood what I'd been missing all those years."

Cat looked at him curiously. "What was that?"

Macon blew a big breath out. "Being a parent is a kind of promise. A promise to stand by someone even if you think they're making a mistake. To love who you get, not who you think you're going to get."

Cat thought about his story. Something was missing. "Why didn't you ever say sorry?"

"A long time ago, I tried. More than once. She didn't want to hear it. For a while, she wouldn't even talk to Lily, which just about broke your grandmother's heart. Slowly, they got back in touch over the phone. The occasional photograph. I never wanted to upset that delicate balance."

She watched him pull a bandana from his pocket. Sometimes Macon was so afraid of doing the wrong thing that it stopped him from doing the right thing.

"At first I thought we'd patch it up. You were born and the years went by. Chicken came along. And then your dad's cancer. It was so fast. And you lost him, Cat—you, and Chicken, and Amanda all lost him."

Macon wiped his eyes.

"When I think about how close I got to never knowing you and Chicken—when I think about all the years I missed that I can never get back . . ."

Cat's eyes filled and the planks of the pier blurred. She willed herself not to blink.

Macon cleared his throat, folding the bandana into a square. "I've spent years being sad and that's enough. Now it's time to make it right."

It wasn't right yet, not to Cat. "You were wrong, you know. Having me was a good thing."

Macon looked surprised. "Well, of course, Cat. I know that. You can tell I know that now, right? Don't hate the fool I was. You and your brother are the best gifts I've ever been given."

She heard his words, but wasn't convinced. Her heart was a balloon. The slightest breeze could send it a thousand miles.

Macon continued, "You can be mad at me all you want. I deserve it. But I'm here to help."

She thought of him that day at the ice cream shop, shredding his paper wrapper. She wanted to be grateful for his help, but a hard lump of sadness sat in the way.

Macon's voice interrupted her thoughts. "I don't mean the contest. I'm your grandfather. I'll be there for *you*—I promise."

Cat knew the truth when she heard it. She reached out, and he wrapped his hand around hers. There was nothing more to say.

They went back to the house and put away the gear. When they stepped into the kitchen, it was like walking into a billowy cloud. Flour surrounded them. Hundreds of biscuits lined the counters, stacked several high on every available surface.

"What in the world—"

"Caterpillar!" Chicken waved the metal biscuit cutter. "We're playing cookiecutter sharks!"

Lily smiled at Cat. "He saw me rolling the dough and wanted to help. I've learned all about cookiecutter sharks this morning."

"Wow," said Cat. "This is a lot of biscuits."

"I'm a biscuit cutter shark!" shouted Chicken.

Macon stepped into the kitchen. "What's this?" he asked.

Chicken held a biscuit in each hand and circled the kitchen in a figure-eight pattern.

"Biscuit cutter shark," he said as he galloped by Macon.

Macon scooped him up. Chicken wrapped his arms around Macon's neck, screaming with glee. "Cuddle fish!"

Macon tossed Chicken in the air. Cat had missed out on eleven years of memories on this island, and Chicken had missed out on seven. But they were making up for lost time. Gingerbread Island was a part of them. And it always would be.

20

Cat studied the detailed drawings on her bedroom wall. Big or small, they were all framed and hung in a perfect spot, fitting together like a puzzle.

There were majestic sailing ships with detailed riggings and portholes, squat tugboats, a pirate ship steered by a mean-looking crew. The maps were of places from books. Cat recognized Middle Earth, Narnia, and the Ozarks from *Where the Red Fern Grows*, all labeled in small, even letters. She was just leaning in for a better look when Lily walked in the open door. She held a basket of laundry.

Cat felt bad that Lily was washing her clothes. "I'll take care of that."

"I don't mind," said Lily. "But maybe you could fold socks and keep me company?"

Socks were the best part of laundry, as long as they all matched up.

"What do you think of your mom's drawings?" asked Lily.

It took Cat a minute. "You mean she drew those? They're different from her style now."

"She'd spend hours getting the details right, drawing as she read. She loved the ships, too—especially ones with ornate carvings. The gingerbread—you know that's what this island is named for?"

Cat nodded.

"Between her books and her drawings, she had an entire world up here with her."

"Did she always like drawing?" Cat asked.

Lily opened the dresser drawer and stacked Cat's shorts inside. "Drawing and painting. Loved to read—like you." She looked at Cat and smiled. "Lots of ideas about changing the world."

"Did she and Macon ever get along?" Cat asked. "They seem so different."

"They're more alike than they think, which is its own kind of problem," said Lily.

Cat considered this. She hadn't ever thought about people being too alike. "How so?"

"Both stubborn, and they love their work a little too much," said Lily. "Macon loved being a surgeon. He wrapped up his whole identity in it—he didn't leave it at the end of the day. He loved his patients too much—and they loved him, too, of course," Lily continued. "Surgeries at the hospital all hours of the day and night. And somehow, in all that busy, he forgot that Daddy's girl was busy, too—busy growing up."

"So he wasn't around a lot," said Cat. "But at least he was alive."

"Your daddy," said Lily as she sank down on the edge of the bed. "I'm sure he loved you to the end of the world and back."

Usually, when people said this kind of thing, Cat walled off her heart. She only talked about Daddy with people who knew him well. People who didn't know Daddy couldn't understand what she had lost. How could she explain him to someone who had never seen his perfect way of peeling oranges or how he danced with Mom in the kitchen?

But with Lily it was different. She knew him before he was her daddy. She said she liked having him visit. Cat twisted a sock.

"I bet he was a great dad," said Lily.

Cat remembered the day in third grade when her teacher explained the idea of infinity. Some kids had a hard time figuring out what it meant, but Cat understood right away. Death was infinity. It wasn't contained in a day, month, or year. It existed in a way that couldn't be measured.

"It's sad backward and forward," Cat said quietly.

Lily paused. Cat realized Lily would wait for hours if Cat needed her to. The thought made her want to keep talking.

"I miss him backward when I think about piggyback rides or cracking eggs. And I miss him forward when I think of all the things he isn't here for, the things he won't ever be here for."

Lily reached out to touch Cat's face. "That's the heart of it, my sweet girl. So sad and so unfair."

Her touch was so gentle, it made Cat's eyes tear. She leaned against Lily.

"I wish someone would have told me I would miss him forever, in all directions."

Lily patted her back. "The weight of the world," she said so quietly, Cat barely heard her. "The weight of the world."

Cat's face was pressed against Lily's shoulder. If Cat kept crying she would make Lily's shirt wet. "I'm sorry," she mumbled. She pulled away, but Lily pulled her back in. They sat like that for a minute. Lily handed her a handkerchief that smelled like lemons.

"Nothing to be sorry about," said Lily.

Cat wiped her eyes.

"I'd make it better if I could. I can't, and no one ever will. But you're welcome to cry on my shoulder anytime. Deal?" Lily asked.

Cat cleared her throat. It was a good offer. "Deal."

Lily hugged her again. Cat would take that, too.

When she let go, Cat picked up the two leftover socks. "I don't have the matches for these."

"I hate that," said Lily.

"Me too," said Cat. "It is the absolute worst."

"Well," said Lily slowly. "Maybe not *the* absolute worst."

Cat looked at her grandmother and they both started cracking up. "Okay," Cat gasped. "There are slightly worse things."

They couldn't stop laughing. Cat folded the mismatched socks together and held them up. Lily started laughing so hard, she was bent over.

Cat caught her breath. "Promise you won't laugh at my mixed-up socks."

"I could never promise that."

They started laughing again. Cat could barely take a breath.

Chicken and Macon were in the doorway. Macon looked worried.

"Everything okay in here?" asked Macon.

"Not really," Cat choked out.

"It's the worst!" Lily howled.

Macon looked at Chicken. "What in the world are they up to?"

Chicken looked at them carefully, then shrugged. "Laundry, I guess."

This made Cat and Lily laugh harder. It was the best kind of worst Cat could think of.

21

Hot peanut butter breath clouded on Cat's left cheek.

"Hello. Hello. *Caterpillar.*"

Cat opened her eyes. Chicken's face was an inch from hers.

She buried her head under the pillow. She wanted her dream back, the zing of her fishing reel in her hands.

He tapped her arm. "Caterpillar. It's me, Chicken."

Cat sighed. "I know who it is."

"Mommy is coming."

Cat peeked out from under the pillow. "But not now. *Tonight.* When we're asleep."

"I know that!" Chicken skipped out of the room.

Cat couldn't wait to see Mom, who had promised they could go fishing. Cat had a plan—right as they headed out the door, she'd invite Macon. That way Mom couldn't say no. Once they were on the pier together, Mom would remember how much she loved fishing—and how much she loved Macon. Everything would be forgiven when the three of them were side by side.

Cat joined Chicken for cereal and orange juice. As they were finishing up, there was a knock at the door. When she opened it, Harriet and Neddie stood there. He waved to Chicken.

"Hey, you guys," said Cat.

"Hey Cat! Want to go to the park?" asked Harriet.

"Sure," said Cat.

Chicken took his bowl to the sink. "Me too."

Cat helped Chicken find his shoes and they went down the white wooden staircase. Right away Cat noticed something was missing. "Where's the sign?"

The Stone House sign wasn't on its hooks. John Harvey better not have taken it. Cat, glancing around, saw Macon stacking scrap wood outside the workshop.

"Do you know what happened to the sign?" she asked.

"Needed fixing," said Macon.

"Did it get a crack in it, Mr. Macon?" Harriet asked.

"Mmmph," said Macon. "Now, you four be careful on your walk. Lots of cars out there today with Independence Day traffic."

They set out together on Ocean Road. Macon was right, the streets were a mess, but sidewalks were okay. At the park, Neddie and Chicken ran to the sandbox.

Without speaking, Cat and Harriet headed in the same direction. At some point they had become the type of friends who knew when a good swing was required.

They picked two side by side and were quiet as they pumped. Before long they were both swinging high. Cat looked over at Harriet, ponytail flying behind her. They would be friends if Harriet lived in San Francisco, Cat was sure of it.

Cat gripped the chains and leaned backward, so she saw only sky. Time passed differently here on the island. A day here felt like a week or even a month in her normal life. She couldn't believe that three weeks ago she had never heard of this place, but now she had memories wherever she looked. The gleaming yellow bicycle. Clouds of flour flying through the air. Sea glass and shark teeth. Fishing with Harriet . . . and Macon.

And Chicken, too. He loved the green plastic laundry basket and finding beach treasures. The way he leaned into Lily. How he listened to Macon.

"Uh-oh," said Harriet.

Cat snapped her head back up, immediately looking for Chicken. He ran in a knot of other kids, chased by a blond boy in a bright orange shirt.

Cat looked closer. "Is that who I think it is?"

John Harvey led the little kids in an elaborate game of tag. It looked like freeze tag but sometimes kids would hold each other's hands and run around connected like that. It must be some special kind of North Carolina tag. Chicken may not have known the rules, but he was running and laughing with the group.

Cat skidded the swing to a stop, keeping her eyes on John Harvey. She couldn't believe it was him. He was careful with the little kids. He smiled a real smile, not the mean smirk Cat was used to.

A little girl with a large bow pulled the hem of John Harvey's shirt. "I got you! Now you have to push."

All the kids screamed with happiness. They piled on the metal merry-go-round. Chicken, with big eyes and a bigger grin, sat on the edge. It made a *screeee* sound as it turned. On one spin, John Harvey jumped on and rode standing up, not holding on to anything.

"Show-off," said Harriet.

Chicken saw the girls and raised his hand to wave. Cat didn't see what happened, but in the next moment he landed on the ground. The spinning metal edge whirled inches from his head.

Cat leaped off the swing. "Chicken, drop and roll!"

He gazed at her in confusion. Then a foot thwacked him in the eye. He rolled onto his back.

John Harvey jumped off and held tight to the railing, stopping the merry-go-round with a jerk. He ran to Chicken and lifted him to standing.

Cat got there a second later and pulled Chicken away. He stood still and breathed in hiccupping breaths. Cat glared at John Harvey. "Don't touch my brother!"

He put his hands up and stepped away.

Cat took a step toward him. "You hurt him!"

That sneer was back again. "I didn't!"

"Then who did?"

The girl with the bow stepped forward. "I think it was my foot. By accident."

Cat leaned down to wipe Chicken's face but he pushed her hands away. "No, Caterpillar!"

"Chicken?" she asked. "What's wrong?" She wondered if his face had been bruised when he fell.

Chicken glared at her. "It's like the library."

Maybe he did get hit in the head, because he wasn't making sense.

Chicken crossed his arms and fixed her with a furious expression. "Why are you so mad?"

His thoughts jumped around so fast, Cat couldn't keep up. "Mad at who?"

"At him!" Chicken pointed to John Harvey. "It was an accident. Like when I hurt Neddie at the library."

"That was different," Cat started, but he shrugged her off.

"I'm going to play," he said, heading right back to the merry-go-round.

Cat was stunned. She looked at her brother, then at John Harvey. Chicken had never been so angry with her.

A bright orange pickup truck came to a stop alongside the park. The side read Dawson Mini Golf. From the side window, Dixie stuck out her head.

A teenage boy leaned out the window. "What the heck are you doing?"

John Harvey's sneer faded. "Nothing."

"Dad sent you to do something, did you get it done?"

John Harvey stalked over to the pickup, muttering.

"Then stop wasting time, we got work to do."

John Harvey put his hand on the side of the truck and leaped in the back. The engine roared as the pickup drove away.

John Harvey didn't have younger siblings, so he had no reason to be at the park. Maybe he was hiding from those brothers of his. If she had brothers like that, she'd hide from them, too. Maybe he liked to play, to be nice to little kids. It was a possibility. But fifteen minutes of being nice didn't erase all the times he'd been mean.

Chicken lay flat on the merry-go-round as it spun creakily. It wasn't easy to keep him safe. Even when she was right there, he found a way to get hurt. But he'd been mad when she tried to help him. Clearly she wasn't the only one who was changing this summer.

22

Cat got out milk and eggs while Lily measured dry ingredients. Mom's welcome breakfast would be waffles. Cat cracked eggs like Daddy had taught her, then whisked. She was surprised to realize she'd missed the rhythm of cooking, the tidy feeling of ingredients coming together. She liked the way the batter sizzled on the waffle iron.

When she heard Mom on the stairs, she ran to hug her. "Mom! I tried to wait up to see you last night, but I fell asleep."

"That's okay." Mom kissed the top of her head. "I'm happy to see you now."

"I'm making waffles," said Cat.

Mom made her plate. "They smell delicious, Cat. Thank you."

Chicken padded into the kitchen and climbed onto Mom's lap.

"Hey, sleepyhead," she said, squeezing him. "What should we do today?"

Cat, distracted, looked over at Mom as she pulled another waffle from the iron. Her finger accidentally touched the hot surface. "Ow!" She put her finger in her mouth. "I thought we said fishing?"

Mom took a bite and swallowed. "I didn't think that was a set plan."

Cat looked at her in disbelief. "I was pretty sure we said fishing."

"Let's do something else. How about ice cream?"

"Yes!" said Chicken.

"I wanted time with you and me," said Cat. *And Macon.*

Mom wasn't listening. "Or—hey, how about boogie boarding? I bet you haven't done that yet."

The whole plan was crumbling. If Mom wouldn't go fishing, Cat couldn't get Mom and Macon together. But maybe if she agreed to Mom's plan, Mom would go fishing later.

"All right," Cat said. "Boogie boarding."

They got in swimsuits and went downstairs. Mom rummaged in the storage area until she found two boogie boards. They walked to the water's edge and waded until the shore was far away.

"Waves are choppy today, huh?" Mom asked.

Cat was about to agree when a wave pounded over her

head. She lost her grip on the board and dunked under. She pushed to the surface.

"You got clobbered," said Mom. "Are you all right?"

Cat caught her breath. "I'm not good at this."

"Don't say that," said Mom. "You're trying—which means you're already better than everyone who never left the shore."

She helped Cat climb on her board again.

"See how the waves crest—see the pattern?" asked Mom. "Don't rush. See what the ocean has for you today."

Cat couldn't help but smile. That patient, teaching voice reminded her of someone else. "You sound like Macon."

Mom's eyes narrowed. "How so?"

Cat winced. Mom didn't think being like Macon was a good thing. "He's teaching me to fish."

Mom paused, and Cat thought she was angry. But after a moment, Mom's face brightened. "That's perfect, then. You don't need me to take you."

That was the last thing Cat wanted to hear. "I still need you," she said. Cat wanted more. She wanted a promise.

But Mom was shouting. "This is it—this is the one! Kick, Cat, kick!"

The wave was cresting, and Cat was in the right place to reach it. With three strong kicks, she caught the wave alongside Mom and they rode all the way to shore. It was better than any roller coaster. It was so fun that Cat put aside her plan. They spent hours in the waves until they had enough.

23

Cat and Harriet weaved their way through the crowds. People filled every inch of the sidewalk and the square. Red, white, and blue decorations covered the shops. The air smelled of popcorn, sugar, and sunscreen.

"I know you said lots of people come for the parade," said Cat. "But this is ridiculous."

"The bridge backs up for miles on parade day. Tourists! At least once they close the bridge tomorrow's fireworks will be island people only," said Harriet. Cat grinned. She was an island person, too.

Harriet found a spot by the judging stand. Patriotic music poured from the speakers. "This is the perfect place to sit. Marchers do their best stuff to impress the judges."

Little kids danced in the closed-off street while volunteers tried to relocate them to the sidewalk.

Something crinkled against Cat's head.

"Hello, Caterpillar." Chicken tapped her with a foil pinwheel.

"Chicken—where's Mom?" Cat twisted around.

Mom waved from several rows away. "He wanted to be with you."

Cat and Harriet scooted over. He squeezed in. "Pa-RADE, pa-RADE, pa-RADE," he chanted, his foil pinwheel spinning.

"Easy, Chicken," said Cat. She wanted to ask Mom if Chicken could go back to her. She turned her head and saw John Harvey behind them. She poked Harriet in the side and nodded her head sideways.

Harriet peeked over her shoulder. "Ugh. Why?" she whispered.

"Who?" Chicken said loudly. "Who are you talking about?"

"Hush," said Cat. "It's about to start."

First came the old-fashioned car with the grand marshal. As it approached, Cat realized two people were riding in it. Two people she knew. Ms. Willis and Dean from the bait shop. And they were holding hands!

Three bulldozers puttered by in a row, decorated with patriotic streamers. Cub Scouts and Girl Scouts carried flags.

Then came the fire trucks—four of them—with lights flashing. At the judging stand, they stopped. Firefighters hopped out and tossed handfuls of candy into the crowds. Everyone stood to cheer and grab at the sweets.

Then the sirens started.

At such a close range, the sound was unbearable. The sounds cycled, screeching and screaming so loud that Cat couldn't hear anything else. The crowd cheered and pushed forward each time more candy was thrown. Cat reached up to try to catch some, but an elbow jabbed her in the back.

John Harvey. He opened his mouth and said something, but Cat couldn't hear.

"What?" asked Cat.

John Harvey pointed at Chicken. "What's . . . wrong . . . with . . . him?"

"What do you mean what's wrong with him? There's nothing *wrong* with him. He might be a little different, but—"

"Cat," Harriet said, grabbing her arm. "Look."

Chicken's hands were over his ears and his face looked frozen, like a scream was trying to find its way out. Tears flowed down his cheeks.

"The sirens. Are they too loud?" Cat put an arm around him and scanned the crowd for Mom. She looked at Harriet, who was frowning, worried.

"We can't move him—too crowded!" said Harriet, talking directly in Cat's ear.

Getting through the crowd would be almost impossible. They were stuck. Usually, when Chicken needed Cat, her brain took over, generating Chicken-helping options like a supercomputer. But that day there was a giant blank. His entire body was rigid, every muscle clenched, and her brain was on lockdown, too.

She leaned down. "It's okay, it's okay," she murmured. He couldn't hear her, not over the sirens and past his hands that tried so hard to block out the world. But it was all she could think of to do. *Mom come find us, soon.*

Finally, the fire trucks rolled on. The sirens still screamed, but soon it would be over. Cat relaxed her arm around her brother.

But Chicken didn't know that. He wrenched away, stepped over the curb, and bolted toward the truck. Cat raced after him. Her brain moved faster than her body as she calculated the speed of the truck, the velocity of her brother, and the precise moment to grab him before he got squashed. With seconds to spare, she leaped and grasped him around the elbow. She yanked him back to their seats.

"Sit here," she said as firmly as possible. "Do not move." She wrapped her fingers around his forearm. He'd better get used to it, because she was going to hold him that way for the entire afternoon.

The fire trucks rolled on, and the sirens faded. Chicken let out a deep breath, like he'd been holding it this whole time.

"Thank goodness," said Harriet.

Cat dabbed at Chicken's face with the edge of her shirt. "You're all right," she said to him as he started to return back to himself. A float with baby sea turtles approached and the crowd cheered again.

Cat, Chicken, and Harriet stayed in their spots on the curb as the rest of the parade streamed by. They saw golf carts with balloons, motorcycles with streamers, three French bulldogs wearing flag bandanas, and a candy-apple-red convertible with Miss Gingerbread Island waving at the crowd. A marching band stopped at the judges' table. Cat held Chicken extra tight, but the music didn't bother him. When it was over, John Harvey disappeared into the crowd. Cat, Chicken, and Harriet stayed where they were. Mom met them with four cups of pink lemonade.

"Cheers," she said, clinking against their plastic cups breezily. "How was it?"

What a question. Cat tipped up her cup so she wouldn't have to answer right away. She didn't know how to explain what had happened with the fire trucks. She knew she'd get in trouble for not watching Chicken closely enough.

"Fine," she answered.

"This lemonade sure is good, Mrs. Gladwell," said Harriet.

"What about you, Chicken?" said Mom. "What did you think?"

Chicken lowered his cup and wiped his mouth. If Chicken told, Cat would be in serious trouble.

"I liked the float with the sharks," he said. "I also liked the dogs wearing clothes."

He wasn't going to tell. Cat crunched her lemonade ice happily and said mental thank-yous—to Harriet for not blabbing, to Chicken for not being any quicker, to the driver of the truck. And one to John Harvey. When he pointed at Chicken, she thought John Harvey was being rude. Maybe he was, or maybe he had been the one to see Chicken needed help. She'd never admit it, but she owed him either way.

24

That evening was braiding night. Cat set up her tablet with one of Mom's favorite movies, the one with the twins, but every two minutes Mom ran into another tangle.

"Ouch, Mom!"

"Sorry," said Mom. "I'll be careful." She began brushing again. She must have been distracted or feeling rushed, because after a few minutes she began yanking again.

Cat pushed away the comb. "Stop pulling!"

"It's a mess," Mom said sharply. "Like you didn't do anything with it the whole time I was gone."

Mom's words hurt more than the comb. Cat switched off the movie.

"I *tried*. You were supposed to be here last weekend to help!"

Mom let out a deep breath. "I know you tried. I was frustrated. Come over here so I can keep going."

Cat didn't budge. Mom was acting like Cat tangled her hair on purpose. And she had called it a mess.

Mom put the comb on a towel and then closed her eyes, pressing her fingers against her temples. She seemed to be thinking about something.

She opened her eyes. "You have beautiful hair, Cat."

Cat shrugged. She wasn't going to let her off that easy.

"When you were small, Daddy did it every week. You sat on his knee and he combed so gently you never complained." Mom gave Cat a quick grin. "Maybe because he let you watch *Binky Bunnies* when he did it."

Cat still knew the words to the *Binky Bunnies* theme song, not that she would admit it. She remembered the way his hands worked through a tangle. She could smell the deep conditioner he used. It smelled like flowers. A few years ago, that conditioner had been discontinued. She'd cried for a week.

Mom picked up the comb absentmindedly and set it down again.

"Having your hair right was important to him, and he knew it would be important to you. He made me understand."

Cat knew all this. After Daddy died, Mom combed and braided. Her fingers had been unpredictable in those early months. Sad fingers were unsteady. Worried fingers pinched.

Sometimes Mom started crying halfway through and they had to stop. But one day it all came together. Mom had learned how to make it tight to keep the braid in but with room for her hair to expand as it dried.

"I'm sorry," Mom said. "For snapping at you. For not being here last weekend to help."

Cat's feelings were still tender. "You called it a mess. It's not a mess—it's *me*."

Mom's eyes were serious. "You're right."

"I need your help, Mom. Will you come fishing tomorrow before you leave?"

Mom looked at Cat carefully. "Is it that important to you?"

Cat nodded.

Mom sighed. "Maybe. If we get up early enough. If traffic doesn't look awful."

That was all Cat needed to hear. She scooted toward Mom, who started brushing gently. When she was done, Cat's braid was exactly the way she liked it.

25

Cat hoped Mom's *maybe* would turn into *yes*, so she packed the fishing gear and waited on the deck. But when Mom came out, she shook her head.

"But I got up early," said Cat. "I got everything ready."

Mom sighed. "I checked the roads. They're already jammed from holiday traffic. If I want to get to Atlanta, I need to get going."

"I do need you, you know," said Cat. "Yesterday you said I didn't need you because I had Macon to teach me, but it's not true. I really miss you. And I want to learn from you."

"I miss you, too," said Mom. "Do you want to come back to Atlanta with me?"

Cat blinked. The idea of leaving Gingerbread Island made her insides feel hollow. She loved the island and the ocean.

She'd found a friend in Harriet and she couldn't bear to think of saying good-bye to Macon and Lily. Plus, the contest.

"I don't know," she said.

"I know it would be long days of watching Chicken, but you could manage for a week," said Mom.

Chicken wouldn't want to leave either, Cat was sure. She had to make Mom understand.

"I love it here, Mom. Chicken loves it, too," said Cat. "Plus, I've been meaning to tell you—the reason I keep asking about fishing is because I entered a contest. It's next Saturday and I've been practicing all the time."

"A fishing contest?" Mom frowned. "Why didn't you tell me?"

Cat thought about her plan to get Mom and Macon together through fishing. That seemed silly now.

"I wanted it to be a surprise," she said. "At first I entered because I wanted to beat that mean kid John Harvey. But I do like it, Mom."

The corner of Mom's mouth turned up in a half smile. "I liked it, too."

That little smile meant a lot. It meant Mom still had good memories of fishing with Macon, even if they were buried deep.

"Will you come early Saturday, to watch me in the contest?" Cat asked.

"Of course," said Mom. She paused, looking at the water. "This place is so magical. It's not that I didn't remember—but everyone thinks their childhood was magical. I didn't know that it would feel this way to me as an adult."

Cat swallowed. "What made you want to leave?"

Mom frowned. "Your grandfather and I had a big fight. It's complicated."

Half the time Mom leaned on Cat, but the other half she shut her out. Cat was tired of going back and forth. Macon had messed up, but Mom had messed up, too. Saying something wrong is one kind of bad. But maybe saying nothing was even worse.

"But he *said* sorry, right?"

Mom's jaw clenched. "I don't want you digging around in that old hurt."

"I'm part of this family, too," said Cat.

Mom took a deep breath. There was something familiar about it, and Cat realized it was what Mom did when she was trying to stay calm with Chicken.

"We can talk about this later," Mom said. "I really need to get on the road." She pushed open the sliding glass door and went inside to gather her things. After a few minutes, Cat went inside, too.

Cat followed the others to the driveway to wave goodbye. Mom gave her a quick hug before getting in the car.

"Bye!" shouted Chicken.

Cat was still thinking long after Mom's car was gone. From what Mom said on the deck, she was beginning to remember what she loved about Gingerbread Island. Maybe at the contest, with a full day of fishing, she'd remember she loved Macon, too.

The night of the fireworks, the streets were closed to traffic. Picnic tables stood in the middle of the square, under strings of white lights. Cat recognized faces from the pier, park, and library.

"I hope you're hungry," said Harriet. "The food is going to be great."

"Course it is," said Neddie. "Dad's cooking." He pointed at Mr. Kincaid, who was carrying a giant pot.

The girls kept an eye on the little brothers while the adults stood in line. Macon returned with a basket and avalanched pink shrimp, corn on the cob, and red potatoes across the paper-covered table. The food was steaming hot.

"Yum," said Harriet and Neddie. They grabbed corn and started eating.

Macon squirted mustard on the table. "No forks, no plates." He dipped a piece of potato and handed it to Chicken, whose eyes were wide.

"Look!" Chicken crowed, flipping a shrimp upside down. "Legs!"

"Gotta peel them," said Neddie, in a businesslike tone of voice. In one quick move Neddie removed the shrimp from its casing and then chomped it down in two bites.

Cat handled shrimp all the time—she didn't blink twice

when baiting her hook. But she had never had shrimp served with the shell on. She nibbled at a potato. Chicken tried peeling one, but ended up pulling his shrimp in half.

"Let me show you," said Neddie. He used his thumb to loosen the shell, then removed it in one piece.

Chicken peered at the shrimp. He tugged the legs until they came away from the body. Then he put a shrimp into his mouth. His eyes widened as he looked at Cat.

"Mrrrmph," he said. He swallowed. "Delicious!"

Cat got to work and after a few tries mastered Neddie's peeling trick. They were delicious—salty and fresh. Soon they had big piles of the shells in front of them.

Cat put her elbows on the table. "I'm stuffed."

"Save room for blueberry cobbler," said Harriet. "We'll get bowls right before the fireworks."

The adults were deep in conversation about erosion on the north part of the island. Chicken and Neddie were still eating. They reached for a shrimp at the same time, and their hands bumped. They frowned at each other and then bumped hands again, and this time, they bumped shoulders, too. Chicken elbowed Neddie, and Neddie elbowed him back, hard.

Cat sat up and leaned toward the table. She felt a hand on her arm. She turned to see, and it was Harriet. "What are you doing?" Cat asked.

"Just wait," she said. "Just see."

The boys locked eyes with each other.

Finally, Neddie dropped his eyes. "Go ahead."

"It's okay," said Chicken. "I'll have a potato." He dunked it in butter. Cat couldn't believe it. She looked at Harriet.

"I figured they'd work it out," said Harriet.

"I thought they'd fight," said Cat. "I didn't want Chicken to give Neddie a nosebleed."

Harriet shrugged. "Fights happen."

Cat shook her head. "It's different for Chicken. He gets upset."

"I know you look after him," said Harriet. "But sometimes letting him handle things is a way of looking out for him, too."

Once Cat heard Harriet's words, she couldn't stop thinking about them—all the way through the rest of dinner, while they were having their blueberry cobbler, and while they watched hundreds of fireworks bursting through the night sky.

26

The next day, Cat was supposed to ride bikes with Harriet, but Chicken was upset.

"Not again," he said. "You always leave. I thought we were going to play sharks or read together."

A cereal flake stuck to his cheek. Cat peeled it off.

Chicken pushed her hand away. "You never play with me anymore."

"Not true," she answered.

"It's not a true fact," he said seriously. "But it's a true *feeling*."

Oh, Chicken. She hated to see him sad. There was a time that his words would have been enough to make her cancel her plans. Being a good sister was important. But sometimes, being a good friend was important, too.

She gave him a little hug. "When I come back, we'll read our book."

When they first came to the island, Chicken chose a dog-eared copy of *Where the Red Fern Grows* by Wilson Rawls. Cat had been unsure, but once they started reading they fell into the story of Billy and his dogs. Chicken loved to whoop during the hunting scenes, just like Billy.

He looked at her like he didn't believe her. "Promise?"

She squeezed him up in a hug. "I triple-promise. As soon as I get back."

He made her promise until she had both quadruple-promised and crossed her heart.

Downstairs, Harriet was waiting.

"Ready?" Harriet asked. Cat nodded.

Harriet tore down the road, and Cat pedaled hard to keep up. The sun shone on the water's curled waves. Cat thought back to the beginning of summer, when she'd been afraid to leave Chicken. It seemed like a long time ago.

They passed the pier and Cat checked for John Harvey. He wasn't there, which was good. The less she saw him, the better.

Past the pier, the path widened and there was enough room to ride next to each other. Harriet slowed until Cat caught up.

Cat hadn't realized the island was so long. The fanciest houses, like Macon and Lily's, were right on the ocean, close to town. Smaller houses like Harriet's were inland a bit. But this part of the island was different. They rode past a swampy area Harriet said was too wet to build on. When houses started again, they were spaced far apart. Some were neat and tidy and others looked abandoned, with boarded windows and tall weeds growing.

They turned sharply on a narrow street and in the distance a mountain jutted two stories in the air. As they rode, Cat got a closer look. It wasn't a real mountain but had been painted to look like one.

She pointed. "What is that?"

Harried grinned. "That's where we're heading. Mini golf!"

Cat's pedaling slowed. "Mini golf?" The course John Harvey's family owned.

"Don't worry, it's my treat," said Harriet. "My mom gave me money."

Cat shook her head. It wasn't the money. She was still sorting out how she felt about what happened at the parade. "Does John Harvey work there?"

"Yeah," said Harriet. "But the course is fun. He won't bother paying customers."

Cat was unsure. They pulled up to a chain-link fence. She looked for a sign of John Harvey.

Harriet hopped off her bike. "Are you coming or not?"

"Definitely," said Cat.

She leaned her bike against the fence. She had a better view of the fake mountain, which actually appeared to be a volcano. Red paint streaked the sides and a lazy curl of smoke ribboned from the top. The course was a colorful jumble of pirate ships, giant butterflies, neon toadstools, and even half a school bus.

Cat looped her fingers through the chain-link fence. "I expected something more basic. Plastic grass, wooden ramps. Not like this."

Harriet nodded. "My mom says that Mr. Dawson is a frustrated genius. He's out here all hours of the night building and painting. My dad hired him for a job once that needed some tile work. It turned out beautiful but went over budget because Mr. Dawson spent a million hours making it perfect."

They walked to the register. A teenager leaned on the counter, tapping at his phone. She recognized him as the one who drove the orange pickup truck at the playground. She could just make out the writing on his fading name tag—Sutton.

Cat stood there, not knowing if she should say something or wait for Sutton to notice them. He was oblivious, even from a foot away. Harriet was low on patience. She reached out and pressed on the bell hard.

Sutton didn't look up from his phone. "What?"

Harriet plunked money on the counter. "We want to play."

Finally, Sutton looked up, shoving the phone in his pocket reluctantly. He reached under the counter to get two putters. Sutton's nose was crooked, like it had been broken and healed funny, but other than that he looked a lot like John Harvey.

Harriet rummaged in her pockets until she found a tattered paper. "Coupon from the *Weekly Wave*," she said, holding it up. "Half off."

Sutton studied the coupon before stuffing it in a drawer. "Old man shouldn't bother running these. We might as well open our doors for free."

He slapped the golf balls on the counter. "Follow the yellow line," he said, pointing at the path. He was back to his phone immediately.

"*Rude*," whispered Cat, after they were out of earshot. But as they rounded the corner, she gasped. There was much more to the course than what she'd seen from the fence. Bright and chaotic, each stop was themed differently. It should have clashed but instead it was fascinating. The first hole was surrounded by a half wall tiled with a mosaic ocean scene. From there she could see the second hole, which was designed like a circus big top, and the edge of the third, which was ringed by enormous lollipops.

After the first few holes, it became clear that Harriet was very good. Cat wasn't—like there was a connection loose between her brain and her hand. She wasn't worried about winning, because they were having fun. She skipped around the corner, but the path was blocked with plastic netting. And even from behind, she knew that floppy blond hair anywhere.

He glanced up at Cat, his eyes narrowing when he recognized her.

"John Harvey," said Cat. "What are you doing?"

"What does it look like?" he asked. "Fixing the path."

Harriet leaned forward for a closer look. "Are you old enough to do that?"

"Guess so," said John Harvey. The corner of his mouth turned up in a half smile, but it was full of pride. "Sutton and Briggs don't have the patience, and Tanner can't stand still long enough to do anything with his hands. My dad's got his other jobs today, so he told me to do this."

The three of them looked at the path. His work looked tidy and even.

"Anyway," he said roughly. "You have to go around or you'll mess it up."

Cat made a face. He didn't need to act big because he could make a sidewalk. Even if it *was* a good sidewalk.

"Obviously," said Harriet. "No need to get bossy. We won't walk on your path." They turned their backs and continued to the pale pink igloo.

When they came to the last hole a great white shark grinned at them menacingly.

"Chicken would *love* this," Cat said.

"On your last ball there's a prize," said Harriet. "If you get it in the shark's mouth you get a token for a free game. See the holes lined up before the mouth? You have to hit it past."

Harriet set up her ball and frowned in concentration.

Finally, she swung. The ball arced over the three holes and landed perfectly.

"Yes!" shouted Harriet, pumping her fist. "Free game!"

"Good job!" said Cat.

Cat put down her ball. She tried to copy Harriet, she even frowned at the ball. One hard swing later, the ball bounced straight into the first hole, not anywhere near the shark's mouth. No prize for Cat.

They returned their clubs at the counter, and Sutton gave Harriet her free token with a scowl. They walked to their bikes.

"Close your eyes and put out your hand," said Harriet.

Cat did, and Harriet pressed something in her palm—the token. When she opened her eyes she shook her head. "No Harriet, you should keep it. We leave Sunday and I don't know if we'll have time to play again."

Harriet grinned. "Exactly. You'll have to come visit another time, so you can use your token!" She ran with her bike, took a flying leap, and began to pedal.

Cat put the token deep in her pocket so it wouldn't get lost. She smiled, not because of the free game waiting for her, but because Harriet would be waiting for her, too. She hurried to catch up with her friend.

After lunch, Cat kept her promise to read. She and Chicken escaped to her cool bedroom and made a pillow nest in the window seat. The chapters blurred into one another as they followed Billy and the dogs deep into the Ozarks on cold winter nights. Chicken pressed so close, she could feel his breath on her arm.

"Cat?" he asked. "Will this book have a sad ending?"

Cat stopped reading and looked at him. "Maybe. Some books have sad endings."

"Caterpillar and Chicken books have happy endings," he said. "I like those better."

"They don't have sad *endings*, but they have sad parts," said Cat, thinking of the drawings of book-Chicken that showed him bursting into tears or erupting in anger. "If she stopped the book at the sad part, there wouldn't be much story, so she keeps going."

Chicken's eyes lit up like he thought of something.

"Wait here!" he exclaimed, padding out of the room.

When he returned he carried the Big Blue Book. Together they turned the pages of their family. There was no need to talk because they knew the story by heart. A few snapshots of Mom and Daddy in college, friends first before they fell in love.

Chicken stared at the photos, finally placing his fingers on one of Daddy grinning at Mom on their wedding day. They stood on the courthouse steps with friends, Mom in a simple yellow dress instead of a fancy white one. He looked up.

"Billy is lucky," said Chicken. "He lives on a farm with two dogs. He has a dad *and* a grandpa."

Cat smiled. "And don't forget, a whole houseful of

sisters—I know you wouldn't want that." She waited for him to laugh, but he was serious.

He glanced at the picture of Daddy again. "What was he like? Was he like Billy's dad?" he asked.

His sweet voice made Cat's insides fold like origami. Chicken had been too little to make his own memories with Daddy. She let him borrow hers.

"He never would have hurt a raccoon. But he liked to build things, and he worked hard, like Billy's dad."

Chicken nodded. He turned the pages, past their parents' cross-country drive and their picture next to the world's largest ball of twine, past baby Cat, past the pictures of her and Rishi as toddlers. He kept turning pages until he got to the ones of him as a baby, which proved how much he looked like a chicken.

But Chicken wasn't looking at himself—he was looking at Daddy, who was already thin and weak. Daddy in a hospital gown, all bones.

Cat wanted to make it better, but she couldn't.

"He got the saddest ending," said Chicken.

Cat nodded. "We all did."

"It wasn't the ending for us," said Chicken. "We have lots of pages left."

It was such a Chicken way of looking at it that Cat smiled. "You're right. We keep going."

Chicken frowned. "Why aren't Macon and Lily in our book?"

"We only just met them," said Cat.

"Oh. Right." Chicken looked across the album at her. They were quiet for a moment, looking at pictures.

"Caterpillar," he said seriously. "I would be sad if you weren't in my book."

She smiled. "Don't be ridiculous. I'll always be in your book."

He pushed his head against her. "Promise?"

She squeezed him close. "Promise."

27

Cat's tablet pinged. She looked up from across the room, surprised. She hurried to the desk and touched the video chat icon. Her friend's face appeared on the screen.

"Rishi!" said Cat.

"Hey!" said Rishi. "Finally!"

"Finally," said Cat. "How is your grandma?"

"She's fine!" said Rishi. "Walking is going to be tough, but she's working hard."

"What is India like?" asked Cat.

"Hot! Crowded! Interesting! Delicious!"

Cat's mouth watered, remembering the way Manjula could cook. "Oh my gosh, the food. Are you eating amazing things?"

Rishi lowered his voice. "Everyone we visit wants to feed me five years' worth of food."

Cat was jealous imagining it. "Have you had those dough-nut hole things?"

Rishi's face looked dreamy. "Gulab jamun? They're even better than my mom's."

Cat laughed. "Lucky."

"It's been a great trip," said Rishi. "I'm so glad we're here. I mean—I'm sorry we didn't get to see you . . ."

"I know what you mean. I've had a good time, too."

"How's Chicken doing?" Rishi asked.

"He's doing great," said Cat. "He loves hanging out with Lily. And guess what—I learned to fish! I'm in a contest next weekend."

"Now I'm jealous!" said Rishi. "Is there a prize?"

"Cash and a trophy," said Cat.

"Oh, man!" said Rishi. "You know if you win, you could buy a plane ticket to Atlanta for later this summer!"

Cat didn't want him to get his hopes up.

"I probably won't win—the same kid wins every year." She thought of John Harvey's sneering face and sighed. He may be an awful person, but she had to admit he was good at fishing.

"Don't be sad," said Rishi. "Even if you don't win, we'll see each other sometime soon."

Rishi told Cat stories about incredible street food in Ban-galore and all his little cousins. Cat told him about Harriet, ghost crab hunting, and what it was like to know Macon and Lily after all this time.

As they said good-bye, Cat was beaming. Sometimes sharing with Rishi made things feel more real. And her time in North Carolina was definitely something she wanted to be real. She wanted to keep it with her forever.

28

Two days before the contest, Cat and Macon sat at the kitchen counter.

Macon pulled a folded piece of paper from his pocket. "Thought we should look at the rules before Saturday."

The flyer was on the same bright green paper as the entry form had been.

GINGERBREAD ISLAND YOUTH FISHING CONTEST

>●> >●> RULES AND REGULATIONS <●< <●<

1. This contest is open to island youth ages 8-14.
2. Tournament time starts at 5:00 a.m. Saturday, July 9. Tournament time ends at 8:00 p.m. the same day.

3. All fish must be caught on hook and line; one
   rod per entrant, which must be affixed to the
   pier or held by the entrant at all times.
4. No assistance may be received from other
   individuals (including baiting).
5. No altering of the environment or pier by
   contestants.
6. Fish must be weighed immediately by official
   contest judge to be considered valid.
7. Prize awarded solely on the basis of overall
   weight of fish caught that day.

Cat looked at the starting and ending times. "That's fifteen hours of fishing."

"You can do it," said Macon.

She knew she could. Over the last three weeks, she'd become stronger, thanks to all the practice.

"I'll be there to keep you company," said Macon. "And I know your fans will drop by—Lily, Chicken, and Harriet."

"Mom, too," said Cat. She smiled just thinking about it.

Macon cleared his throat. "I wanted to mention something. There was a challenge to your entry because you don't live here year-round."

Cat, worried, met Macon's eyes. All her work would be for nothing.

"I didn't mean to worry you," Macon said. "You aren't considered a tourist because Lily and I live here full-time."

"Who challenged my entry?"

Macon folded the paper in thirds. "Dean didn't say."

Cat had an idea of who it was. What did John Harvey have against her anyway?

"I'm proud of you, Cat—you've worked hard."

"I want to win," said Cat.

"I know you do," said Macon. "I know."

PART FIVE
Before & After

Adventure's not all it's cracked up to be.

—Caterpillar in *Caterpillar & Chicken: Rainbow Roller Coaster*

29

Lily clucked under her breath. "That man is going to drive me to distraction."

Macon stood outside, neck craned toward the sky. It was the afternoon before the fishing contest and it looked like rain. Macon was monitoring the situation. First, he looked at the wall barometer. Then he loaded his phone's weather map. Finally, he walked outside to check the sky. Afterward, he came inside. A few minutes later the cycle repeated.

In the evening, Macon backed the blue Jeep out of the driveway without saying where he was going. Cat half wondered if he was driving to the mainland to find a meteorologist to discuss things with.

She was reading in her bedroom when Lily came in. She handed Cat a gray plastic bag. "From your grandfather."

Cat opened the bag. Inside were a rain hat and pants in her size, in bright yellow.

Cat touched the slick, waterproof material. "That was nice."

"He wants you to have a good chance tomorrow."

Cat didn't want to let him down. "Do you think he'll be disappointed if I don't win?"

"Not at all." Lily straightened the quilt. "Will *you* be disappointed?"

"Yes," Cat admitted.

Lily kissed Cat's forehead. "Big dreams of prize money, huh?"

It wasn't just the prize, but Cat nodded anyway. Lily left, closing the door softly behind her. Cat turned her pillow to the cool side.

She couldn't wait for Mom to see how much she had learned. Mom would have to know it was all because of Macon. It meant he had learned to keep promises. Mom wouldn't have to be mad anymore.

They'd visit Gingerbread Island every summer, and Macon and Lily would visit San Francisco. Macon would admit he'd been wrong about how he'd reacted. Mom would admit she'd carried a grudge for too long. They would be a family again. And Cat was the one who could make it happen.

30

Cat chewed each bite a hundred times. Her throat was dry and her stomach was full of little jolts of electricity. She'd barely slept the night before.

Macon sat across from her. "All set?" he asked.

Cat nodded. "I packed the rain clothes—thanks for that. I double-checked the gear last night."

She managed to eat half her sandwich and then they closed the door on the still house. They'd fished many mornings, but today leaving the house felt different. The next time Cat was at the house, it would be as a winner or loser.

She looked at everything as they walked to the pier—towels spread over deck railings to dry, funny little windows with flowery curtains, an orange kayak left upside down to drain. She would remember it all.

A crowd of people milled around the pier. An electric-green food truck, painted all over with fish, was parked at the pier entrance. The pier lights gave the morning mist a ghostly glow. Dean stood in the center of everything. Macon and Cat set down their gear and joined the cluster of people.

Fourteen kids were entered. Five were girls. The youngest kids looked sleepy, the middle kids like Cat looked excited, and the older kids looked bored. John Harvey was there, of course, standing next to Briggs. Up close, Cat noticed he had long, straight eyelashes just like his brother's. Briggs's hand snuck out in a lightning punch to John Harvey's ribs. It happened so quickly, Cat would have missed it if she hadn't been looking right at them. John Harvey stayed silent but rubbed his side gingerly. Cat had a flash of that same feeling she had when she met John Harvey that day on the beach—that he was someone who needed protecting. But it faded as she remembered the mud on her bike and his taunts about the contest.

Dean tapped on a bucket and the crowd stilled. "We are about to begin the annual Gingerbread Island Youth Fishing Contest," he announced. "Welcome!

"As you know, our co-sponsor for the event is the Small Fry food truck." Dean gestured to the truck. "As for logistics, all fish, after being weighed by the judges, will be delivered immediately to the truck for preparation and serving. Part of the day's proceeds will be used for the prize money. Thank you, Small Fry, for your generous support of our event."

Everyone clapped and the chefs from the food truck bowed and waved.

"We must go over the rules—I know, the boring part," he said. "We don't expect there to be any problems with the rules this year." He looked around and Cat may have imagined it, but his eyes seemed to stick an extra second on John Harvey and Briggs.

Dean read in his deep voice. It was the same list she and Macon had read. Cat looked at the other contestants. Most had at least one parent with them. She was glad Lily, Chicken, and Harriet would cheer her on. Mom would be there soon. She wondered if anyone besides Briggs would come for John Harvey.

Cat looked up at Macon. He listened to Dean and took small sips of coffee. He told her he would stay by her side all day, but she wouldn't blame him if he needed a break. Fifteen hours was a long day. But almost as if he could hear her thoughts, Macon looked at her and smiled the smile that crinkled his whole face. The smile said he would stick with her, just like he promised.

Dean said, "And with that, we wish you luck. Contestants, take your places!"

Cat was so nervous, she didn't remember how to hold her reel. All the contestants took their places on the pier. John Harvey made a beeline for his lucky spot at the end.

With only fourteen contestants and a long pier, there was no reason to fight over one spot or another. In fact, Cat planned to move throughout the contest. She would watch the birds and water for clues. For now, in the dark, this was as good a place as any. She baited her hook with a small shrimp and waited for the opening bell. Even in the cool morning air, her palms were sweaty.

BUZZ! Fourteen lines lowered into the water.

Cat's nervousness faded. Weeks of hard work and preparation took over. She grinned at Macon. After weeks of planning, she was finally where she wanted to be.

The crowd was quiet and full of anticipation. Who would catch the first fish? Minutes passed.

A whoop rang from the end of the pier. She couldn't believe it! John Harvey reeled one in. An official carried the fish to the judging tent, then a minute after that, a bell rang. The fish had been weighed, recorded, and was on its way to the food truck.

"Don't let that rattle you," said Macon.

As the sun came up, eight fish had been caught, two by John Harvey. It was hard not to be discouraged.

"Gonna wander," said Macon. He strolled to the judging tent and chatted with the officials. When he returned, he explained that the large whiteboards listed a running total for each contestant.

"Am I behind by much, Macon?" asked Cat.

"You've got nowhere to go but up," Macon said.

Suddenly, her line zinged. "Macon, I've got one!"

She reeled it in slow and steady, like she'd practiced. It

was a red drum, heavy as anything she'd ever caught. The official took it to be weighed, Macon following behind. *RING!* When he came back, he was smiling.

"Four pounds!" he told her.

"Awesome!" She had already re-baited, hoping for another bite quickly.

Midmorning, after a few more catches, Macon suggested she take a break. He watched her gear while she went for a walk to stretch her legs.

She checked out the menu board. The types of fish were listed along with the name of the person who caught it. Cat's red drum had a line through it because it had sold out. John Harvey had a few crossed out on the board. She saw some other names of contestants she didn't know: Luis, George, Annabel, Ella. Smaller fish, like spots, were sold in a single serving. The woman working the counter saw her looking at the board.

"Hey," she said. "Hungry yet?"

"I'm fine," said Cat. "Maybe later."

"Contestants eat for free, you know," she said. "These hush puppies just came out." Without waiting for an answer, she pushed a cardboard tray across the counter. The hush puppies were lumpish, with a sweet, greasy smell.

Cat returned to her spot on the pier. She showed the hush puppies to Macon, who pinched one immediately.

"Macon? What are these exactly?"

"Never thought a granddaughter of mine wouldn't know

what a hush puppy is!" Macon laughed. "It's fried cornmeal. Try it."

That didn't sound like much, but Cat took a bite. Crisp on the outside and fluffy inside, they were a bit like cornbread but they were so much better. She reached for another.

"Glad you like them." Macon laughed again. "You're making up for lost time."

Macon had been joking about making up for lost time, but in another way, that described exactly what she was doing. She'd made the most of her time on the island, and in return she'd been given so much.

The tide rolled in. Cat remembered what Macon always said about reading the day. She baited her hook with a mole crab and dropped it in the water, letting it sink to the sandy ocean floor. Slowly she retrieved it, hoping its motion would make a fish curious. Her line pulled. She reeled it in quickly and then repeated the same strategy again and again.

"You're on fire!" Macon exclaimed. The nearby official laughed.

"We might as well set up a chair here," he joked. "Busier than a moth in a mitten!"

"That's my granddaughter," said Macon, beaming.

He strolled to the whiteboard and then returned. "You're in the top four."

"Is John Harvey in first?" Cat couldn't resist asking.

Macon nodded. "I'm a bit puzzled as to how he's ahead by so much."

"He's won the last four years," said Cat. "I'm sure he'll win it again." She took a deep breath and pushed it out slowly. "But we're halfway through the day. Fourth is not that far from first."

Chicken stomped down the pier, sneakers lighting up, calling: "Caterpillar! Caterpillar!" He was a burst of questions. "How's the fishing? How are the fish?" He pointed at his shirt. "See what I got?"

He was so excited to show her his "I'm a Reader" ribbon from the library reading program.

"Wow, Chicken, did you get a prize?"

He nodded vigorously. "And they gave me a book about sharks! Don't worry, I will let you borrow it."

"Cool," said Cat. "Thanks."

Chicken wrinkled his forehead. "I wanted to read and play on the statues, but Lily said we had to meet you. And I came without a fuss."

She gave him the biggest one-armed hug she could manage while still holding on to her fishing rod. "I'm impressed. You're getting so big."

Chicken beamed.

Macon turned to him. "Let's you and me rustle up some lunch." He held Chicken's hand as they walked to the food truck.

Cat turned to Lily. "Have you heard from my mom? She should be here soon, right?"

"I just got a call . . . she said she was held up."

Cat's smile faded. "When will she be here?"

"Not until late, I'm afraid," said Lily. "She said not to wait up."

Cat shook her head, wishing away the tears that sprang up in her eyes.

Lily studied Cat's face, concerned. "I know she wanted to be here."

"Wanting isn't enough," said Cat. "She promised."

"I know you're disappointed." Lily squeezed Cat's shoulder.

It was more than being disappointed. It was seeing her plan fall apart. Mom would miss the contest. If Mom wasn't here, she wouldn't see how important fishing had become to Cat. She wouldn't see Macon, patient and steady. The plan would never work.

If she thought about it any more, she might burst, so she changed the subject instead. "Do you think we'll get that rain today?"

Lily pointed at a row of clouds in a line just behind the row of houses facing the beach. "The ocean breeze is pushing them back."

"Hope they stay away," said Cat. "Although Macon might be sad if I don't use my rain gear."

Lily reached out and squeezed her again. "Cat, we love having you here."

Cat hugged her back. "Me too!"

"I want it to feel like another home to you," said Lily. "A soft place to land. Everyone can use another one of those."

An idea popped into Cat's head. "Do you think sometime I could invite my friend Rishi? He really loves fishing, and I know he'd love it here."

Lily squeezed her hand. "Of course! Anytime."

Her heart shone with love—for the island, for Lily and Macon, for Mom and Chicken, even for airplanes, which made the whole world a few hours away.

Chicken proudly carried a tray of hush puppies. Macon was right next to him with a platter of fish, more hush puppies, and cups of sweet tea and lemonade. Cat affixed her line to the pier. The flavors and smells were all just right. Luckily, Macon brought a lot of napkins.

"Small Fry is doing a good business today," said Macon. "There's a big crowd waiting."

"Caterpillar, your fish are delish!" said Chicken.

They ate and ate. Chicken slurped at the last of the lemonade.

Lily kissed Macon's cheek. "We'll visit this evening." She kissed Cat, too.

Lily and Chicken walked the length of the pier and across the sand to the path. Lily held Chicken's hand in just the right way.

Macon asked Cat how she was doing. "Do you want to walk the pier?"

"All right," said Cat. They said hello to other contestants when they passed. At the end of the pier, John Harvey was reeling in a big one. Briggs was with him, and Sutton, from the golf course.

"Dumb luck, John Harvey," said Sutton.

Briggs spat on the pier. "Nothing to do with luck."

Cat looked at Macon, who shrugged. The boys bragged about the weight of the fish. Cat and Macon walked away.

"What did he mean that it wasn't luck?" Cat scrunched her forehead, thinking. "Maybe he meant John Harvey doesn't need luck because he has so much skill."

"Fishing's at least half luck," said Macon. "The way I do it, anyhow."

Cat moved to a spot on the pier about halfway between two other contestants.

Several pulls on her hook came in a row. She looked at Macon. "That was weird," she said. "It tugged a bunch."

Macon raised his eyebrows. "And what do you think of that?"

Cat imagined the fish in the water, not giving a neat pull but a few. "I think the fish is getting a grip on the bait. I should wait until it's set and bring it in real slow."

Macon's eyes crinkled with pride.

Cat waited for the tugs to stop, then slowly pulled in her line. Eventually she saw a flat brown fish at the end of it. She'd never caught one, but recognized it anyway. "A flounder!" she said.

"I thought it might be," said Macon. "They take a bit to set up on the hook."

A judge came over to take her flounder. When Macon returned from the weigh station he told her the weight.

"You may not be catching the most fish," said Macon. "But you've been catching some nice big ones, and that'll pay off. And thinking like a fish makes you unstoppable."

Cat grinned at him. This was about the highest praise she could ever get, she was sure of it.

While she baited the hook, Macon told her he needed a walk. She watched him disappear into the crowd before dropping her line.

After a few moments she heard a voice calling. It was Harriet, along with an older boy. He was tall, with dark brown hair and as many freckles as Harriet. It had to be her brother.

"Walt got back from camp this morning," Harriet said.

"Hey," said Cat. She remembered that she and Harriet had used his equipment in the early days of learning to fish. She should thank him.

"Thanks so much for—" Cat started, but then stopped as Harriet caught her eye and shook her head wildly. Oh, right. They hadn't had permission to borrow the equipment, exactly. Cat shouldn't blab. But what could she thank him for, if not the gear?

"Thanks for coming to see me in the contest," she finished awkwardly.

Walt looked at her sideways. "Later." He wandered off.

Cat and Harriet burst into giggles.

" 'Thanks for coming to see me'? When you've never even met him? He probably thinks you're in love with him," said Harriet.

Cat groaned. "I can't believe I said that."

"He would freak if he knew we used his gear," said Harriet.

"I know! I forgot!" said Cat.

"Oh well," said Harriet. "A minute of awkwardness is better than hearing him complain for my entire life."

It was easy for Harriet to say. Cat peeked over her shoulder and saw Walt and Luis talking. Briggs stopped to talk to him, too.

"Is Walt friends with John Harvey's brother?" Cat asked.

Harriet shrugged. "They're in the same grade."

Walt returned, shaking his head.

"What happened?" asked Harriet.

"Briggs is positive John Harvey will win," said Walt. "He wanted to make a bet."

"Is he winning now?" asked Harriet. "Never mind, he probably is."

"He is," said Walt. "By a pretty big amount."

"I don't get it," said Harriet.

"Me neither," said Walt.

Raindrops spattered to the ground. "Uh-oh," said Walt, looking at the sky. "It looks like that storm is rolling in after all." He and Harriet left, Harriet promising to return later.

The afternoon wore on, the rain light but steady. Cat was glad to have her rain gear. Macon held his umbrella over Cat's head to keep her dry.

"Are Lily and Chicken coming back?" Cat asked.

"Not if this rain continues. They'll wait up for you at home."

Cat checked her watch. Only four hours left until the contest was over. John Harvey had maintained his lead. Cat, Luis, Ella, and George were all in the running for second place.

Macon walked down to the food truck and returned with more fish and hush puppies. "There was a little of your flounder left, so I got that," he said. The fish was hot and flaked when she bit it.

"Nothing like fish you caught yourself," Cat said.

Macon dunked a hush puppy in sauce. "Couldn't agree more." They sat under the umbrella and looked out at the gray ocean.

"Thanks, Macon," said Cat. She wanted to thank him for keeping her company in the rain, but the words got all tangled up inside her. She thought of the bicycle. The fishing trips. Talking on the pier, side by side. The way his face looked when she caught her first fish. She swallowed.

"I'm the one who should be thanking you," he said quietly. "For the best three weeks since I don't know when."

"Me too," said Cat. There was nothing more to say.

Shortly after dinner, Harriet returned, wearing an orange raincoat and polka-dot boots. "Can't believe this rain," she said. A couple of contestants left. Their names stayed on the board with their totals.

"Guess they knew they couldn't catch up to John Harvey," said Harriet.

"Do you want to bow out?" Macon asked Cat.

"I'm not afraid of the rain," said Cat. "And my luck might turn around." The words were barely out of her mouth when she felt the tug on her line. It felt like the heaviest fish Cat had ever caught. Her arms ached as she pulled it in.

"Spanish mackerel," said Macon. "A huge one!"

"I'm going to see how much it weighs!" Harriet exclaimed. She went to the judging tent. *RING!* When she reported back, she told Cat it weighed over five pounds.

"Wow," said Cat. "That's good."

Harriet and Macon stood with her as she brought in a spot and another flounder. The judging official didn't come over for the flounder. They looked around. The tent was empty. At the end of the pier was a small knot of people. She couldn't see John Harvey. "What's going on?" asked Cat. "Did John Harvey catch a big one?"

"Can't tell," said Macon. The rain made it hard to see. There was a movement in the crowd and some raised voices. Then the activity quieted. The cluster of people parted. Briggs came first, his hands shoved deep in his pockets. He looked around, glaring, and took fast steps. John Harvey came next. His face was red and he looked at the ground. Whispered conversations bubbled up the moment they were out of sight.

"What in the world?" asked Harriet.

"We'll find out soon enough," said Macon.

The judges returned to the tent. Harriet said, "I'm going to have a listen."

Harriet sidled up to the tent and leaned against it, every cell of her body straining to hear. Finally, she hurried back and ducked under Cat's umbrella.

Harriet's eyes were wide. "John Harvey was disqualified!"

"*What?*" asked Cat and Macon, together.

"He broke a rule. It sounded like they were saying that he put cinder blocks in the water at the end of the pier. Why would he do that?"

"Ahhh," said Macon. "He created an artificial reef."

Cat looked at Harriet, who shrugged. "An artificial reef?"

"Fish love little nooks and crannies," said Macon. "A reef creates an area where fish can grow and thrive."

Harriet let out a low whistle. "That's pretty smart."

"Smart and illegal," said Macon.

Cat and Harriet exchanged looks.

"*Illegal?*" asked Cat.

"It breaks the contest rules and island law," said Macon. "It's a bit of a mess."

"He broke the law?" asked Cat. "So he's in trouble with the *police?*"

"There might be a fine of some kind, I suppose," said Macon.

"They don't have money to pay a fine," said Harriet. "Maybe he'll have to go to jail."

Harriet had said they barely had enough to keep the golf course running. Cat didn't know how much a fine would cost, but it was probably a lot.

Macon read the question in her eyes. "It's all right, Cat. He won't go to jail."

"That's why he had a lucky spot," said Harriet. "He made it lucky."

"That's why Briggs was so sure he'd win," said Cat.

Harriet clapped her hands. "Those boys got what was coming to them. They're bad all the way through. I'm going to tell Walt." She zoomed to her brother.

Macon studied Cat's face. "What do you think?"

Cat fiddled with the reel. She should be happy, but she was all mixed up.

"John Harvey was the whole reason I entered this contest in the first place. I haven't liked him since I saw him playing on the dunes," she said.

Macon frowned. "It's against the law to play on the dunes. It hurts the plants and animals."

"That's what I said!" said Cat. "But also, I was worried that he would get hurt. His brothers were kicking him."

Macon nodded, waiting for her to go on.

"Only, I thought he was a little kid because he's short. I think I embarrassed him, but I was trying to help. He's been mean ever since, like I made him look bad on purpose. He was the one that put mud on my bike, I just know it."

Macon rubbed the side of his face thoughtfully. "Harriet says he's bad all the way through—what do you think about that?"

Cat didn't know what to think. It was easier to think of John Harvey as one thing—a bad kid. But when she thought of his smirk she also saw his wide-open smile with the playground kids. His scratchy voice bragging about fishing trophies was the same voice that warned her about Chicken at the parade. The truth was that John Harvey wasn't one way or the other. He was good and bad, at the same time.

"I used to believe in people being all bad or all good," she said. "But now I don't. Most people are good and bad all mixed together."

Macon looked prouder than when she'd pulled in the mackerel. They stood like that for a moment, listening to the waves.

Harriet's footsteps pounded on the pier. "Cat! I checked the board. With John Harvey gone, you have a chance to win!"

Cat held up her hand. "Don't tell me the numbers. I don't want to know."

Macon smiled to himself. "Attagirl," he said quietly.

The only thing to do was wait.

The sky pinked and the sun set. Before she knew it, the final bell clanged. She had caught many more fish, but was it enough?

The contestants circled the judging tent. The rain turned to a drizzle. Macon held the umbrella above Cat and Harriet.

"First off, the judges and I are proud of you contestants," said Dean. "All y'all have shown dedication to the great sport of fishing. We are most pleased to see the future of fishing on Gingerbread Island." The crowd applauded lightly. Harriet whistled.

"The first prize we'd like to announce is a specialty prize, the Small Fry prize—for our youngest contestant participating today. Lucas Winters, come on up here." A short boy with glasses and missing teeth walked proudly to the center of the circle. Dean handed him a small trophy and shook his hand. "We thank you for your participation, Lucas." Everyone applauded.

"We'd also like to take this opportunity to thank the Small Fry food truck for their sponsorship and support. The top three winners will receive a cash prize: one hundred dollars for third place, three hundred dollars for second place, and for our grand prize first place winner—five hundred dollars!" There was lots of clapping and whistling.

Harriet leaned over to Cat. "Did he say five *hundred* dollars?"

Cat closed her eyes. She hoped she would be in the top three.

"In third place . . . Ella Patterson."

Ella bounced up to shake hands with Dean.

"In second place . . ." Dean smiled big as he read the paper. "Cat Gladwell!"

Harriet screamed and pounded her back. Macon whistled and stomped his feet. Cat was frozen. They'd read her name! Finally, Harriet gave her a little shove.

When she made it to the front, Dean pumped her hand, then handed her a shiny trophy. It was heavier than she thought it would be. Cat stood next to Ella and listened to Dean announce that Luis Bustamante, Walt's friend, had won first. He held his hands up over his head like a prizefighter, which got some laughs. After shaking Dean's hand, he took his trophy and lined up with the girls.

Cat leaned over to Luis so he could hear her over the cheers. "Congratulations, Luis!"

He smiled back at her. "You too, Cat—you too, Ella!"

The crowd held up phones and cameras, flashes snapping, cameras beeping. A reporter from the *Weekly Wave* had a big camera and a bigger flash. Cat felt dazed. When the pictures were done, Macon and Harriet were waiting for her.

"You did it!" said Harriet.

"Attagirl!" said Macon, hugging her.

Harriet reached out her hand. "Let me see that shiny thing." Cat passed her the trophy.

"It's enormous!" Harriet pretended to stagger under the weight.

As they talked, Dean and Ms. Willis came over. Dean shook hands with Macon and Cat.

The rain drizzle turned into drops, and Cat figured they would have to head back to the house soon. She didn't want the night to end, but the rain was determined to stop it.

"I don't know why we're all standing around in this rain," said Macon. "What do you think, Cat? Could we head back home and rustle up some hot chocolate for this crew?"

"I'll get Walt," said Harriet as she dashed off to get her brother.

They walked without hurrying, even though the rain was coming harder.

Macon recalled the events of the day, eyes sparkling with pride. "Remember that big one toward the end? The mackerel?" he asked.

"The huge one!" Harriet exclaimed.

"Oh, yes, that *was* a big one! Almost six pounds," said Dean.

Macon's eyes crinkled. "When Cat reeled it in, I thought that it looked about as big around as she is!"

Macon might not consider himself a fisherman, but he sure knew how to brag like one. It felt good to hear him talk about her like she was the greatest gift to fishing the state of North Carolina had ever seen.

Cat's cheeks hurt from smiling. Second place wasn't what she had dreamed of, so why was she so happy? After the day of fishing, her arms ached and her legs were like jelly. She was sore, she was tired, she was soaked. And she was happy.

She looked at Macon. He had moved on to a different story, eyes sparkling, hands sideways to show how big the fish had been. He saw her looking and squeezed her shoulder in a one-armed hug. If this is what second place felt like, Cat would take it every time.

31

Macon whooped and hollered as they approached Stone House. The other Kincaids joined them, and the driveway was crowded with people laughing and talking. The screen door upstairs snapped open. Cat held the trophy behind her back.

Lily hurried down the stairs and looked back and forth between Cat and Macon. They both managed to keep a straight face.

"Well?" Lily finally asked.

Cat held her trophy in the air, beaming. "Second place!"

Lily squealed and clapped before enveloping Cat in a warm hug.

"She did great, stayed focused on her goal," said Macon.

"You'd never gone fishing until you got here. Look at you now," said Lily.

Cat thought back to the day she arrived—when she decided she and Macon would never have anything in common. A lot had changed. "I couldn't have done it without Macon."

He shook his head. "You're tenacious, Cat—you know how to dig in and fight for something you want."

Lily beamed at them. Her eyes looked shiny, too. She cleared her throat. "That reminds me," she said to Macon. "Didn't you have something you wanted to show Cat?"

Macon wiped his hands on his shorts and went to his workshop.

The rain around them changed from a patter to a pounding. A puddle of water collected in the driveway and Neddie stomped his feet. He wore rain boots and owl pajamas. "Where's Chicken?"

"He fell asleep on the sofa," said Lily. "We'll wake him in a bit."

Macon returned, carrying something large and heavy. It was the wooden sign for the house—the one that said The Stone House.

Cat was confused. She knew the sign had been down, but she wasn't sure why he wanted to show her. "You fixed the sign?"

Macon brought it closer, and she saw. Underneath the thick letters were two new carvings. To the left was a chicken. To the right, a cat. The chicken looked playful and happy. The cat was serious and strong. Cat traced the grooves in the wood. She was Cat, not Caterpillar. Somehow, Macon knew.

"I fixed it," said Macon. "Or, I guess you could say that you and your brother did."

Her happiness warmed her to the end of each finger and toe. Macon hung the sign and everyone clapped.

Dean rubbed his hands together. "Now, how about that hot chocolate?"

Cat was up the stairs two at a time. She couldn't wait to show Chicken the trophy. She walked softly so she wouldn't startle him. The sound of the rain was just as loud as it had been outside, and wind howled through the open sliding glass door.

Cat frowned. That door was never left open. She turned to look at Chicken on the sofa. She wanted to see him snoring and sweet, tucked under one of Lily's quilts.

But he wasn't there. The couch was empty, except for the twisted quilt and a small plastic shark with chewed-up fins.

"Chicken?"

Cat looked around the room wildly. Cold fear prickled the back of her neck.

"He's not here."

The group was still coming in the kitchen door, but Lily heard her. She crossed the room quickly and looked at the sofa. "The bathroom?"

Macon frowned, concerned. "No, I was just there." He paused for an instant, thinking. "I'll check the bedrooms."

His feet thundered up the stairs. Cat clutched the plastic shark. A breeze blew through the open door. He definitely would be upstairs. Another silly mix-up. She heard Macon's feet moving from room to room.

He called out, "He's not up here! Lily, he's not here!" The chill from the open door grew stronger.

Lily stopped. "The basket was here when I left. Where is it?"

It wasn't there. Together, they looked at the sliding glass door. Was it open wide enough for a scrawny seven-year-old to fit through? A seven-year-old who thought he was a shark researcher, carrying the laundry basket he thought was a boat?

Ms. Willis pulled out her phone and started dialing. "I'm calling search and rescue." She began speaking in an urgent tone to the operator on the other end of the line.

She caught Lily's eye. "What was he wearing?"

Lily bit her lip. "Blue pajamas, with sharks."

The floor felt uneven. Cat thought she might throw up.

Macon crossed the room in two steps. He slid the glass door wider and stepped onto the deck. Dean and Mr. Kincaid were right behind him. As if it were happening from very far away, she heard Mrs. Kincaid tell Walt to knock on the neighbors' doors. Walt raced out the door in a blur.

"Neddie and I will search upstairs," she said. "We'll double-check the closets and under the beds." She paused, looking at Cat. "We'll find him, honey. It will be okay."

They dashed up the steps before Cat could answer. He wouldn't be upstairs, Cat was sure. A horrible thought occurred to her. She couldn't get in enough air to breathe right, but she had to talk. She looked at Macon and forced the words out.

"He has his boat," she said. "He would have gone straight for the waves." She had to find him. She went to the door.

"No." Macon's arm stopped her. "Stay here."

The others headed down the stairs and onto the beach. Lily handed out flashlights—the same ones they had used hunting for ghost crabs.

"I'm going," Cat insisted. She pushed into Macon.

He blocked her firmly, looking her in the eye. "No kids on the beach."

She pushed again. "I'm not a kid."

Macon's jaw squared. "No, ma'am. A kid is exactly what you are."

She struggled. When he spoke, his voice was loud and commanding.

"NO, Cat. We can't risk losing you. Don't make me waste time arguing. Get off the beach."

Cat knew he wouldn't budge. If she tried to make a break for it, he'd chase her instead of Chicken. Macon was her brother's best chance—stubborn Macon, who'd walked the beach every day and knew it better than anyone.

She looked at her grandfather. "Bring him back, Macon. Please."

He was already turning toward the roaring ocean. "I promise!"

With these words, he sprinted across the sand until he

disappeared into the night. Flashlight beams scattered down the shoreline. Over the pouring rain and howling wind, the adults shouted Chicken's name.

She watched through the sliding door, looking so closely, her nose pressed the glass. The dark and rain made it impossible to tell which of the figures were Macon and Lily. Others joined the search and began walking farther up the beach. Cat wasn't sure where they had come from.

As if she had read Cat's mind, Harriet spoke. "Someone sent an Island Alert. My mom or Ms. Willis, probably."

Cat turned to Harriet. "But they got here so fast."

Harriet nodded. "On the island, we work together to survive. Waiting for help from the mainland would waste time."

Cat realized she was gripping Chicken's toy shark. The fin dug into her palm. A whine of sirens echoed from far away.

Harriet's freckles stood out against her pale skin. "You don't know that he went to the water."

"I hate this waiting," Cat said. "I wish I could *do* something. Anything."

"You know," Harriet said, looking at Cat out of the corner of her eye. "Macon said no kids on the beach. He didn't say you couldn't leave the house."

Cat swiveled to look at Harriet. Her friend was a genius.

"Can you think of anywhere else to check?" Harriet asked.

Cat had to think like Chicken—something she could do better than anyone.

The memory of their San Francisco afternoon bubbled to the top of her brain. Chicken loved books. Gingerbread Island didn't have a bookstore, but—

"The library," she said. "He told me he wanted to play on the statues, but Lily made him go to the pier."

Together they bolted for the kitchen door. They flew downstairs, made a sharp left, and charged toward downtown, running through the rain.

Cat's thoughts swirled. She felt the sensation of her life splitting into a Before and After, like the Before and After of Daddy dying. If Chicken was lost, her life would be forever divided by this night. All of her Before life would be on one side. The other side, past the moment of losing Chicken, would be After. If he was lost, she could never get back to the Before. Her life would never be whole again.

The sirens grew closer, until a fire engine roared past. Would the sirens scare Chicken? Should she direct the firefighters? Cat wavered for a moment, but Harriet pulled at her sleeve.

"My mom will wave them in," Harriet said. "We have to check downtown."

Cat nodded and they kept running. They reached the library and saw at once that Chicken wasn't there. Harriet pointed to the top of the library steps, where the roof extended: a shelter from the surging rain. When they reached the top, Harriet jiggled the door, but it didn't budge. She kicked it in frustration.

Cat had let herself believe they would find him. Until then, she'd been able to force the idea of Chicken in the waves from her mind, but now it was like he'd been lost all over again. She wanted to cry, scream, or hit something. But mostly she wanted her brother—his light-up sneakers and his no-tear shampoo, his shark facts and his airport meltdowns.

"Chicken!" Harriet screamed. "Chicken!"

From the top of the steps they could see all of downtown. Miss Sunshine's ice cream had closed. Willis General's lights were turned off. No one was out for a walk in the storm.

Harriet's wet hair was plastered to her forehead. "Is there anywhere else?"

Cat squeezed her eyes shut. The rain pummeled the roof and splashed the steps. She couldn't keep her thoughts straight. There was an odd sound in the distance, but it wasn't thunder.

Cat frowned at Harriet. "Do you hear that?"

Harriet tilted her head. A metallic sound arced over the storm. *Screeee, screeee, screeee.*

The girls turned to each other.

"The playground," said Cat. "Let's go."

Their sneakers squished as they ran across narrow streets, around a bicycle, and into the park. The merry-go-round spun, but Chicken wasn't there. It was John Harvey.

Cat wanted to cry. She stepped toward him. "What are you doing here? Don't you know it's raining?"

John Harvey gave her a look but didn't say anything.

Of all the faces in the world, she couldn't believe she was seeing his. It was so unfair. He was always in the way.

"Let me get this right: You got kicked out of the contest and instead of going home like a normal person, you sit on a merry-go-round in the pouring rain?"

John Harvey pushed his hair away from his eyes. "I saw the alert about your brother and I thought I'd look for him. I know he likes the playground."

Lightning arched through the sky, followed immediately by a crack of thunder. Startled, Cat clapped her hands over her ears.

"That's real close," said John Harvey. "Dangerous."

They went through the gate. John Harvey hopped on his bike. "I'll look for him on the way home. You better go back."

He pedaled away, splashing through deep puddles.

"Come on," said Harriet. She wrapped her arm around Cat's shoulders like she was protecting her, hurrying without running. Every time the lightning lit up the street, Cat gasped. She couldn't believe she was returning without Chicken. If Chicken was out in the storm, he would be so scared. She hoped they'd found him, hoped she'd see his little face in the window.

They rounded the corner. The fire truck parked out front flashed its lights. Every lamp in the house was on, and unfamiliar cars filled the driveway. A small car screeched to a stop in the street. Mom jumped out.

Her eyes were wild. "Why is the fire department here? Are you okay?"

"I'm okay," said Cat. "But—"

"But what?" Mom's panic was rising, ready to fall off the edge. "But what?"

Cat opened her mouth but no words came out. She tried again. "Chicken."

Mom grabbed Cat's shoulder. "*What*? What happened?"

"Mrs. Gladwell," said Harriet. "Chicken's missing."

Mom raced up the steps, the girls following. Inside was warm, dry, and quiet. Mrs. Kincaid stood by the sliding door. Walt read a book to Neddie and a few other small kids Cat thought she recognized from the playground.

Mrs. Kincaid saw them first. "You're back! Thank goodness."

"Have they found him?" Mom asked. Her voice was small and scared.

Mrs. Kincaid shook her head slowly. "I'm so sorry. They haven't."

Mom pushed the sliding door and raced outside. Cat went to follow, but Mrs. Kincaid stopped her.

"You promised your grandfather," she said. She hugged Cat and Harriet even though they were soaked.

"It will be okay," said Harriet. "It has to be."

Harriet meant well, but she didn't understand. There were no guarantees in life. Cat leaned against the glass, staring at nothing. She did not want to know what it felt like to grow up without him. She did not want to miss him in all directions.

"Go get some dry clothes," Mrs. Kincaid said.

Cat and Harriet looked up in protest.

"I know you don't want to, but I'm the mom on the premises and I say you have to. It won't do any good for you to sit here shivering."

Cat didn't have energy to argue. She climbed the stairs silently, changed into sweatpants and a hoodie. She grabbed some dry clothes for Harriet out of the clean pile waiting to be packed.

Cat thought of packing—and unpacking. She hadn't looked at her suitcase since the day Macon had met them in the driveway.

She frowned. It couldn't be.

Her feet barely touched the stairs. She crossed the kitchen to the refrigerator. On the wall, a row of hooks, each with keys dangling.

Except one key was missing.

Cat checked again, forcing her eyes to slow down. She searched the shiny white counter. She looked across the floor. No key.

With each step to the elevator, her hope grew.

There it was. The key in the lock.

She pushed the button. She did not think. She did not hope.

With a muffled *ding* the elevator doors slid open. Inside was a green laundry basket. Inside the green laundry basket was a boy in blue pajamas. He looked at her and blinked. Outside, thunder rumbled.

"Hello, Caterpillar," said Chicken. "Want to go on a boat ride?"

32

Cat didn't have the words to explain to Chicken why she was hugging him so much. But if it were up to her, she wouldn't let go for days.

"This is too much hugging," he finally said.

She loosened her grip, but only a little. "We thought you were lost, Chicken. I'm so glad you're safe."

Mrs. Kincaid went to the deck and shouted to the rescuers.

The first one inside was Mom.

She ran to Chicken and scooped him right up.

He squawked in protest. "Why are you squeezing so hard?" He squirmed, but she wouldn't let him go.

"I can't believe you disappeared like that. I've never been so scared." She looked at his face like she was trying to memorize it.

Chicken craned his neck. "Where did all those people come from?"

Cat turned to look. The other rescuers flowed into the house. She hadn't realized that a crowd of islanders had showed up to help.

Lily popped through the glass door and made a line straight to Chicken. Her eyes were brimming with tears. First she kissed Chicken all over his face, and then she pulled Mom and Cat in so all three hugged him at the same time. Chicken complained that the hug was wet and sandy, but Cat didn't mind a bit.

Macon came over next. He reached his square hand to the top of Chicken's head and patted him so gently it was like a butterfly landing. His expression was full of sweet relief, and it made Cat remember all over again how much they might have lost.

But when he turned to Cat, his arms were wide. He hugged her so hard, her feet left the floor. He twirled her in a circle before setting her down again.

"You found him! You saved the day!" He beamed at her and Cat felt the warmth of a thousand suns.

People came over to see Chicken and talk to Mom, Macon, and Lily about how they were glad he was safe. Before long, Macon was at the stove preparing an enormous pot of hot chocolate. Lily fussed at him, trying to wrap him in a quilt—but he refused. He said he'd never felt better.

Cat found out why Macon was so soaked. On the beach,

he thought he'd spotted Chicken in the ocean, so he raced right in.

"That was something," said Dean. "Never knew he could move so fast." It was easy to laugh because Chicken was safe and they were all together.

"Of all the things," Lily fretted. "Thought you saw him in the waves. You'll get pneumonia if you aren't careful." But she was laughing, too, and her eyes shone with love.

Half the island was there. The kitchen didn't have enough mugs, so they improvised. Ms. Willis had her hot chocolate in a jelly jar and Dean swigged from a soup bowl. There was enough to go around for everyone.

Cat had looked the scariest future in the eye and had been rescued from it at the last second. She had landed someplace soft. She had landed here.

As the rain quieted, kids yawned and the crowd began to trickle out. Ms. Willis hugged Cat close. "I'm going to miss you, baby girl. But no one on earth will miss you as much as your grandfather. Come see us soon."

Harriet stood in front of her, frowning. It was the same frown Cat misunderstood the day they first met. Now she knew it was a thinking frown, a trying-not-to-get-upset kind of frown.

Harriet hugged Cat so quickly, she barely knew it had started before it was over. "I'll see you tomorrow, so I won't say good-bye today." She nodded firmly and stepped out the door.

Then it was just the five of them. Mom and Chicken sat

on the sofa. Macon swept the sandy floor while Lily gathered piles of quilts and towels.

"That's the last of them," said Lily. "I think I'll get a load started before bed."

Mom stood. "I think we'll be leaving tonight, actually."

Cat's stomach tumbled. Leaving *tonight?* "Mom—what? I thought we would leave tomorrow."

Mom shook her head tightly. Her mouth was in a straight line. "This was a bad idea. I never should have dropped you here. They lost Chicken—we could have really lost him this time."

Lily had a hollow expression. "Amanda, please stay. All of you. We'll talk about it in the morning. We've had such a good visit. Let's not end it like this."

"No," Mom said firmly. "We tried, and it didn't work out. You should have been more careful."

Mom looked at Cat. "Pack your things."

Cat couldn't believe it. First Mom dropped them in a place where they didn't know anyone, and now she wanted to rip them away from it. The idea of not seeing the island again—not seeing Macon and Lily—made her insides smash.

Mom's jaw was square, like she had made up her mind. But Cat had made up her mind, too.

"No," Cat said. "I'm not leaving."

"Me neither," Chicken chimed in. He stood as tall as he could, and crossed his arms.

Mom blinked like she couldn't believe what she was

hearing. "Kids, you have to understand. It's my job to keep you safe. I can't have Chicken running off like that. He didn't go into the ocean, but he could have."

Cat looked at Macon. She wanted him to help her. He looked like he had already lost.

"Please, Macon," she said. "Do something."

Macon cleared his throat. "Amanda, don't leave like this. Not again."

Mom shook her head furiously. "This is all your fault, Dad. You weren't here for me, and when I gave you a chance with your grandchildren, you weren't around for them either."

Macon took a step back.

"Mom," said Cat. "That's not fair."

"You don't know what it was like," Mom said. "He was never here. It was like I didn't have a dad at all." As soon as the words were out, she clapped her hands over her mouth, like she wanted to put them back in.

For a moment, everyone was still—even Chicken.

When Cat spoke, she did so slowly. "I know exactly what that's like, Mom. Maybe he was away a lot, but it's not like it is for Chicken and me."

"I didn't mean it like that," Mom started. "I meant to say that he was never . . ."

But she saw the look on Cat's face, and stopped talking.

"He might not have been there as much as you wanted, but he was still yours," Cat continued. "I saw the pictures. He loved you."

Mom let out a short cry. "I wish I could take that back. You're right—it isn't the same at all. I'm so sorry."

Cat was surprised. Mom rarely apologized. But the apology was like a bandage on a wound that needed stitches. Cat had to go on.

She took a deep breath. "It wasn't Macon's fault, or Lily's fault. It was mine."

But Chicken was shaking his head. "Stop, Cat. That's not right. It was my fault."

"What do you mean?" Cat asked.

"No one made me do it," Chicken explained. "So it's *my* fault. I feel bad when I scare you."

Cat stared at him. He looked brave, standing in those blue pajamas that were too short in the leg.

"So why do you run?" she asked.

He shrugged. "Sometimes the idea of *going* is so strong, I can't think of anything else. It's like my other ideas get crowded out."

She'd never thought about how he felt when he ran, only that it scared her. She should have asked him earlier if he could explain.

Mom looked at Cat carefully. "Why would it be your fault that he ran away?"

"Not that he ran away," said Cat. "But my fault for not telling you it's been happening. He ran off at the parade. And back home—I lost him on Clement Street the day before our trip."

Mom looked stunned. "But Clement Street is so

crowded—the buses, the traffic. Anything could have happened." She shook her head as if to clear it. "You should have told me."

"I'm sorry." Cat let out a raggedy breath. "I didn't want you to worry when you were working. But it's happened a lot this year."

Mom looked back and forth between Cat and Chicken. "A *lot*?"

Chicken looked at the floor.

"I see," Mom said. Sometimes Mom didn't notice a thing. Other times, she could see through walls.

Cat wanted her to understand. "But on the island, he's been doing a lot better. Except tonight. And, technically, he didn't leave the house."

"I wasn't running," Chicken said. "It was more *exploring*." He nodded like that explained everything.

Mom rubbed the sides of her head like she had a headache. She looked at the stairs. Cat was afraid she would pack everything up and whisk them away from the island. If only Chicken hadn't picked that day to disappear.

Macon reached for Lily's hand. She wasn't sure if he was giving strength or borrowing it.

"I get that you don't need them," Cat said quietly. "But did you ever stop to think that Chicken and I might *want* them? They belong to us as much as they ever belonged to you."

The room was quiet. Chicken yawned loudly, then took a few steps toward Macon, who scooped him up automatically.

"I'm going to bed," said Cat. "I'm not leaving until you

guys figure things out. You are the grown-ups, so you better act like it."

She stomped up the stairs, half expecting a voice to call her back, but none did. She collapsed into bed. It felt like she'd been awake for an entire week.

Her brain tried to convince her arm to reach over and turn off the light, but her arm wasn't interested. There had never been a tired so tired as this.

There was a gentle tap at the door and Cat opened her eyes. It was Lily.

She sat on the edge of the bed, studying Cat's face. "Are you warm enough? You must have gotten quite a chill running around out there."

"I'm okay," Cat said.

Lily pulled up the blankets the way Cat liked and then turned off the light.

"Good night, sweet girl," Lily said in a voice as warm and rich as hot chocolate.

"Lily?" Cat asked. "Are they talking?"

Cat could feel Lily smiling in the dark. "They are."

"Good." Cat snuggled in the quilt, her pillowcase smooth and slippery against her cheek. She was almost asleep.

When Lily reached the doorway, she paused.

"I've been thinking," she said. "Sometimes holding a family together is not a quiet kind of work. Sometimes it's exactly the opposite."

The door clicked shut and Cat grinned until she fell asleep.

33

Mom sat at the table with a cup of coffee. When she saw Cat, she looked up. "Hungry?"

"Not really."

Mom said, "Do you want to sit outside?"

Cat nodded. They stepped into the cool morning. There was a quilt on the porch swing. "Let's sit here," Mom said.

They sat and rocked together. *Crick, crick, crick,* went the porch swing. The waves rushed in and out. The rhythm was comforting and familiar. Cat remembered how weird it had seemed when Mom had breathed in the salty air. Now she breathed deep herself. She didn't know that a place could get to you like this. That a place could be a kind of friend to you, in a way. She would be sad to leave it.

"Can I put my arm around you?" Mom asked, her voice

shaky. Cat nodded. Mom cleared her throat. "What a night, honey. I'm so sorry."

Cat nodded. "You shouldn't have tried to make us go."

"I know." Mom sighed. "I was out here all night."

Cat was surprised. "By yourself?"

Mom shook her head. "With your grandfather. And Chicken."

Cat's eyes widened. "Chicken got to stay up all night? That's not fair."

Mom smiled. "No, no. He fell asleep when my dad was holding him, and neither of us had the heart to set him down. So Chicken slept in his arms." She wiped her eye.

"But why were you awake all night?"

"We had a lot to talk about," said Mom. "He had some things to apologize for . . . so did I. We have a wall between us that's built over time—from before I was your age."

"Did you break it down?" asked Cat.

Mom let out a short laugh. "Let's say we chipped away at it. But the point is, I learned something from listening to him, and from remembering my part in what happened."

Cat looked at the waves. The water was choppy.

Mom continued, "When I was growing up, he was gone a lot. Now, he thought he was doing the right thing by providing for us, and maybe he was. But the truth is, I felt like he never saw me for who I was. I was his pretty Amanda, his sweet Amanda, almost like a pet—or a toy. I hated that feeling. And when he came face-to-face with who I was . . . with what I wanted . . . he couldn't handle it. He couldn't handle *me*."

"What you wanted? You mean Daddy?"

Mom reached over and touched Cat's cheek gently. "Yes—Daddy—but all of it, really. Being an artist, living in San Francisco—having you. That's what I wanted my whole life, my every dream come true."

Cat thought of the rainbow of colored pencils, the drawings of ships with their detail and power, the maps of imaginary places. The room was the room of an artist, a girl who wanted to sail out of this life and all its expectations.

"Obviously," said Cat.

Mom laughed again. "It wasn't obvious to him—he about hit the roof."

"Sometimes parents aren't the best at seeing their kids, I guess," said Cat.

Mom squeezed Cat's shoulder gently. Cat leaned into her. "Sounds like you might know how that feels."

"Sometimes," Cat said. They swung like that for a while.

"Dad said something else last night," said Mom. "He was a little worried about history repeating itself."

Cat made a face. "I'm not going to elope, Mom. So gross."

Mom laughed. "Not about that! About me working too much. About me not being there like I should be. Not letting you be a kid enough." She reached over and touched Cat's hand. "Is that about right?"

Cat nodded. "Yeah. That's right. I mean, I like to help but—"

"But you need some time to be a kid," Mom finished.

Cat remembered the night before, when Macon stopped her from running on the sand, telling her she was just a kid. She nodded.

"We'll make changes," Mom said. "They won't be perfect. We have to keep talking to each other so we can figure it out. And the second we figure it out, you'll grow up a bit more and we'll have to talk again. But I've got some ideas to get us started."

Cat pushed off the deck to make the swing go faster. "Uh-oh. Like what?"

Mom laughed. "For starters, I think Chicken should try the after-school care program next year when second grade starts."

"I'm not sure," said Cat.

Mom blew out a big breath. "Honestly, I'm not sure either. But I think we're ready to try."

Cat thought about this. She remembered what Harriet said on the Fourth of July, about letting Chicken have a chance to work things out. She nodded.

"And maybe your own room?"

Cat's eyes widened. "Really? What about your studio?"

Mom smiled. "I'll figure it out, sweet Caterpillar."

Her own room! Maybe they could paint the walls the same gray green as her bedroom here. She would ask Lily the name of the color. But there was one thing that was bothering her.

"Mom—no."

Mom's eyebrows wrinkled. "You don't want your own room?"

"I don't want to be Caterpillar anymore."

Mom took a deep breath. "I see. Even at home?"

"Not anywhere," Cat said. "Well, Chicken can call me that, but he's the only one."

"I'll try," Mom said finally. "I will try if it's important to you."

Cat wanted her to understand. "I don't want to feel like I'm a character in your book. Especially not that character."

Mom gave her a slight smile. "Is Caterpillar all that bad?"

Cat let out a short laugh. "That's the whole point. She's the opposite of bad! And she always gets the raw end of the deal."

Mom nodded. "In some ways you *are* Caterpillar to me. There is such good in you and that's what Caterpillar is . . . every good thing . . ."

"I noticed!" said Cat.

Mom smiled a little. "But Caterpillar isn't who I want you to be. Caterpillar is who *I* want to be. The mom I wish you both had."

Cat leaned against her. "I don't want a caterpillar for a mom."

Mom hugged her close. When she looked at Cat, her eyes

were wet. She pulled the quilt around them. "I want every perfect thing for you."

They leaned back against the swing and looked at the water together. As the swing *crick*ed a hundred *cricks*, Cat thought about the summer and all the disappointments and surprises it had brought her. Nothing had gone like she expected.

"You know," Cat said, leaning against Mom's shoulder. "I'm starting to get the idea that perfection might be overrated."

The morning was spent on the beach. Everyone felt tired from the night before, but the tension had cleared. Macon and Mom sat together for hours watching Cat and Chicken make sand castles and find the last of their beach treasures. It wasn't fishing, but it was just right.

After lunch, Harriet knocked on the door. She and Cat went downstairs and stood in the driveway, talking.

"I wanted to say good-bye," said Harriet. "This summer will be boring without you."

"Can't be true." Cat grinned. "You're about the most fun I person I ever met."

They exchanged contact information and then gave each other a giant hug.

The elevator dinged and Macon stepped out with the suitcases. Cat noticed that the key was now in Macon's pocket, not on a hook. He nodded at the girls.

Harriet pedaled away, then did a sharp U-turn. "I forgot!"

"Forgot what?" asked Cat.

Harriet hopped off the bike, pulling an envelope from her back pocket. "For you."

Cat examined the envelope. CAT was penciled on the front in square letters. She felt bad she didn't have something for Harriet.

"You didn't have to do that," Cat said.

Harriet shook her head. "It was on your bottom step when I came upstairs to say good-bye. I put it in my pocket and forgot it was there."

"Oh!" She felt the envelope. Whatever was inside was heavier than a letter.

Harriet frowned. "I better go before I get real sad. Tell Chicken I said good-bye!" She ran her bike down the driveway and jumped on, pedaling fast.

Cat tore the envelope. She couldn't believe what she saw. She held it up. "Macon, look!"

His eyebrows furrowed. "Now, who could have found that?"

Cat held the metal license plate in her hands, feeling the bumpy letters that spelled out Mom's name. There was only one person who would have delivered that envelope. One person who was not all bad and not all good, but somewhere in between. Just like Cat.

She looked up. "I need to take one last ride."

Macon looked at his watch. "You've got about thirty

minutes. Better skedaddle before Lily sees you, or she'll hug on you 'til the car is half out of the driveway."

Cat didn't need to hear another word. She pedaled past pretty pastel houses, past the fishing pier, past the swampy field. She was looking for her enemy. She was looking for John Harvey.

34

Cat kept track of where she was by the smoke from the fake volcano. Harriet had said John Harvey lived past the golf course. She didn't know what she would say, but she needed to find him.

The house on the road was very small. The paint peeled, but except for that it looked nice, like someone took good care of it. A low white fence ran around the yard and the orange truck was parked out front.

Before she could change her mind, she opened the gate. She knocked and waited. The door opened when she was about to give up.

A woman stood there, clinging to a walker. She was old and fragile, like a paper doll. She blinked in the sun.

"Hello," the woman said. Her voice was pleasant. "Can I help you with something?"

"Sorry to bother you," said Cat. "I'm looking for John Harvey."

"He's not here," she said slowly. "He might be at the golf course."

"Thanks," said Cat.

The woman closed the door.

Cat had lost some of her nerve. She decided it was better that she didn't see him. She opened the gate and latched it behind her. Then she heard a sound she would have known anywhere.

"Yip! Yip!" Jingle, jingle.

It was Dixie, running down the road as fast as she could toward the little white house. John Harvey was right behind her.

Cat reached down to pet Dixie, who rolled over to show her furry belly. "You're such a softie," said Cat.

John Harvey came closer. "Hey."

Not mean. Not nice, either.

"Hey," Cat said back. She straightened up.

Dixie shook herself, tags jingling.

"Why does she need so many tags anyhow?" Cat asked.

John Harvey shook his head. "What do you want?"

Cat didn't know where to start. "Your grandma said you weren't home."

His shoulders tensed. "She's not my grandma," he said flatly. "That's my mom." He unlatched the gate and Dixie scampered onto the grass.

"Oh!" said Cat, flustered. "I thought—"

"I know what you thought." He closed his eyes for a second, then opened them again. "She's sick. Sometimes her muscles don't work right, makes it hard for her to move."

Cat always clashed with John Harvey, even when she didn't mean to. She hadn't wanted to be rude. "She seemed nice."

John Harvey took a giant breath and blew it out slowly. "Why are you even here?"

She might as well ask. "Listen, about yesterday . . ."

John Harvey turned to her, hands jammed in his pockets. "Did you come all this way to make fun of me for sitting in the rain? Or to call me a cheater?"

"No, would you listen to me for one second? I wanted to thank you for searching for Chicken. He was fine—he was in the house the whole time."

John Harvey nodded. "In the elevator. I heard."

Cat sighed. He was not going to make this easy on her. "Someone said you might have to pay money or something, like a fine. I wanted to see if—if you needed some."

John Harvey shook his head and his hair flopped around. "Number one, I'm not taking your contest money. Number two, I already got it worked out. I'll be doing community service until I'm an old man, but I don't have to pay a thing."

Cat breathed out. "Okay. I was worried."

John Harvey squinted at her. "Worried about me?"

Cat held out her thumb and forefinger so they were almost touching. "*Slightly* worried. Barely."

His smile spread in slow motion. Cat noticed for the first time that one of his ears stuck out more than the other. "Do you always worry about people who are *the worst*? I thought the best thing about me was my dog."

Cat shifted uncomfortably. It didn't feel good to hear her words from the day on the pier with Harriet. She'd hoped he hadn't heard her, but he definitely had.

"Yeah, well. I still think you're awful, John Harvey. But maybe not completely."

Dixie trotted up with a slobbery tennis ball. John Harvey took it from her and bounced it down the road. "Maybe you have a point. Cheating is pretty awful."

Dixie dashed after the ball and trotted back like she was confident she was the world's best dog. She dropped it at their feet.

"The idea was pretty smart, actually," Cat said. "Except it broke the rules."

John Harvey nodded and tossed the ball farther. Dixie raced back and dropped the ball for Cat. She tossed it.

John Harvey watched Dixie hurry for the ball.

"Listen," he said slowly. "On second thought, I *will* make a deal with you."

Cat latched her helmet, looking at him carefully. "What deal?"

"Let's say you come back next year and win first place . . ."

Cat sat on her bike. She imagined the ocean, the pier, the fish pulling her line. "Yeah, let's say that happens."

He squinted a smile in her direction, with only a touch of sneer. "THEN you can give me all your money."

Cat almost laughed. He was impossible.

"What?" she said. "You're saying second-place money isn't good enough for you, but first-place money is?"

"You got it." John Harvey looked pleased with himself.

She shook her head. "Nope. No deal."

Dixie barked her yip-yip bark. That dog had an excess amount of energy.

Cat pushed off from the curb. "Bye, Dixie."

John Harvey protested. "Wait! No deal on coming back next year? Or no deal on giving me your money?"

Cat was blocks away and he still called after her.

"Deal or no deal, Cat Gladwell?"

"No deal, John Harvey!" she yelled back.

The car was packed and ready to go.

When Lily saw Cat, she brightened. "I have something for you."

She handed Cat a drawstring bag no bigger than her hand. Inside was a necklace with a sea glass pendant in the exact shade of the Atlantic the day Cat first saw it.

Cat looked at Lily. Lily said quickly, "I want you to have it. So you always remember."

Cat hugged her. "I could never forget."

While Lily fastened Cat's necklace, Macon lifted Chicken in the air, making him shriek with happiness. He set down Chicken and opened his arms for Cat.

Cat wrapped her arms around Macon in a big hug.

"I'm going to miss you. Thank you for teaching me so much!" she said against his chest.

Macon's voice was a rumble. "Likewise, kid."

They let go.

"Maybe you could come visit us," said Cat.

"Now that's an idea. It's time for me to see what I've been missing." He caught Mom's eye and winked. She smiled and then they actually *hugged*. Cat was shocked. If someone had told her three weeks ago that Mom and Macon would be hugging good-bye, she wouldn't have believed it. Maybe there was something magical about Gingerbread Island.

Macon handed Cat an envelope. "Open it when you're on the road, okay?"

Cat nodded. They had their luggage, and all their treasures. It was time to go. They waved good-bye.

As they drove down Ocean Road, Cat soaked up the colorful houses, the town square, and the ocean breeze. It hadn't been the summer Cat was expecting. But in some ways it had been the best summer ever. Next to her, Chicken was peeking in his own silk bag from Lily. He held up a shark tooth that had to be three inches long.

"It's huge," he breathed, holding it in his hand.

Cat touched its edge. "Perfect, Chicken. With all those teeth you collected, you could open a shark dentist office."

"That doesn't even make sense," he complained.

Cat remembered Macon's envelope. Inside was a picture from yesterday, at the fishing contest. Lily had snapped it at lunch. Macon's arm was around Cat's shoulders. They squinted and grinned at the camera with the green ocean behind them. Macon would be in her book. She was in his. There was no doubt about it.

"Can we come back again next year?" asked Chicken as they crossed the swing bridge.

"I think that can be arranged," said Mom.

Cat smiled. Another year, and another fishing contest. More time with Harriet, the queen of fun. Another chance to beat John Harvey doing something they both loved. She touched her necklace and looked at the photograph on her lap. Another chance to stand side by side. She couldn't wait to show up on Gingerbread Island again.

ACKNOWLEDGMENTS

I had a lot of help.

Laura Case saw me through the entire process. She was my first reader and my biggest cheerleader, and she told me when I needed to kick it into gear and *send already*. I am thankful for her friendship. She makes the world a better place.

Thank you, Marietta Zacker, for your insight, encouragement, and tenacity. I am glad to have you in my corner. Thank you to Nancy Gallt and all at Gallt & Zacker, especially Erin Casey, who loved Chicken first.

Many thanks to Bloomsbury Kids. Mary Kate Castellani is this book's best friend. Her editorial eye made the book (and me!) stronger. Thanks also to Claire Stetzer, Erica Barmash, Anna Bernard, Bethany Buck, Alexis Castellanos,

Regina Castillo, Phoebe Dyer, Beth Eller, Alona Fryman, Emily Gerbner, Cristina Gilbert, Courtney Griffin, Melissa Kavonic, Jeanette Levy, Erica Loberg, Cindy Loh, Donna Mark, Elizabeth Mason, Brittany Mitchell, Oona Patrick, Emily Ritter, and Lily Yengle. Alisa Coburn, thank you for the gorgeous artwork. I am in awe of your talent.

Chris Kleinschmidt, Anna Shartzer, Alice Pierce, Robin Hall, Kirsten Bock, and Anna Totten gave invaluable feedback. Everyone should be so lucky to have a bearded librarian, and Keith Hayes is ours. Thank you for talking the finer points of biscuitry with me.

Caroline Flory is a gifted writer and a true friend. She helped in countless ways. (Thanks to Peter and Grace, too!)

Thank you to the members of the 2019 debut group, with extra special thanks to Chris Baron, J. Kasper Kramer, Rajani LaRocca, Cory Leonardo, Josh Levy, Naomi Milliner, and Nicole Panteleakos.

Wes Hall assisted with fishing scenes. Special thanks to Larissa Marantz, Brandie Harris, and Michelle Stepp for help with authenticity. Any mistakes are my own.

I'm thankful for the friendship of the entire Kavadias family—Carrie, Jaidyn, and Elijah. Thanks for letting me ask questions.

In seventh grade I had the enormous fortune to land in Jackie Skahill's English class. She believed in me then and never stopped.

Rebecca Petruck provided endless encouragement and a

terrifically timed writing weekend. Thank you, Amy Phariss, for many well-spent days.

Sixteen years ago my dog made friends with Gauri Johnston, and dogs are always right about people. I talk to Gauri about almost everything, including several scenes in this book. She made many contributions but my personal favorite is her assertion that Manjula would have given the kids dosas for their after-school snack.

Thank you to my treasured friend Aislinn Estes, who helps me be a better person.

Thank you to my family for supporting my writing.

My husband, Jon, teaches me the importance of showing up. He also peels my oranges and strings twinkle lights above my desk when I'm having a rough day. Marrying him was the smartest thing I ever did.

Nora, Leo, and Violet are my dreams come true.

Thank you, everyone. I am lucky.